How to Make Paper When the World Is Ending

By Dallas Woodburn

Published by

◤ köehlerbooks™

3705 Shore Drive
Virginia Beach, VA 23455
800–435–4811
www.koehlerbooks.com

HOW TO MAKE PAPER WHEN THE WORLD IS ENDING

DALLAS WOODBURN

VIRGINIA BEACH
CAPE CHARLES

For my brother Greg, who told me,
"Patience is a bitter seed that bears sweet fruit."
Thank you for helping me keep the faith that this fruit would come,
and for celebrating the journey with me along the way.

TABLE OF CONTENTS

STORY TO TELL AROUND A CAMPFIRE

The first thing to do is look around the campfire and assess your situation. Do you want to tell a scary story or a romantic one? Who is your audience? What are your goals here?

Either way, the story begins like this. A young man asks a young woman to go away for a long weekend with his family. They've only been dating for a few months, so this is a *big step*. The guy's parents and brother, who the young woman has not yet met, will be there. They have rented a cabin in the countryside. It is springtime; the wildflowers are just beginning to bloom.

"Everyone wants to meet you," the young man says. You should probably give him a name at this point. Something unobtrusive, unthreatening—Mark, perhaps.

The young woman—Hannah, or something like it—is surprised by the invitation, but delighted. She thinks she might love Mark, and this invitation must prove that he is beginning to love her, too.

"Yes!" she says. "I'd love to come!" And they hug and kiss, hungrily.

They leave on a Friday. It is a long drive to the cabin, and Hannah watches out the window as the urban landscape fades away to rolling green hills and cow pastures. They turn off the main highway, and for the final hour the road winds dizzily up through the mountains. Hannah, carsick, rolls down the window to let the breeze in. If this is a romantic story, the breeze smells refreshingly like pine. Describe the way the sunlight filters through the trees like a spotlight indicating loveliness—a moss-draped log here, a clutch of orange poppies there. If this is a scary story, describe the way the tall trees press up against the narrow road, leaning in, their thick branches blocking out most of the sunlight. The breeze is cold and sends a chill down Hannah's bare arms.

The cabin sits back half a mile from the main road in a graveled clearing of pines. Mark parks the car behind his father's Jeep. He insists on grabbing both his and Hannah's suitcases from the trunk and carrying them, one in each hand, into the cabin. He smiles and tells Hannah it is not a problem. Yet, she notices how the veins on his forearms accentuate beneath his skin. The front door is unlocked, and Hannah opens it.

"Hey, guys, we're here!" Mark calls, but the house is still and silent. He sets the suitcases down in the hall. "*Hell-ooo*? Mom? Dad? Johnny?"

He walks through the rooms, calling out for his family, but there is no response. Hannah, unsure whether to remain in the entryway, follows him through the cabin.

If this is a romantic story, focus on the vases of red and purple wildflowers; the seashells and driftwood lined up on the windowsills; the cozy indoor fireplace and neatly folded, hand-crocheted blankets on the couch. If this is a scary story, mention the cabin's quirks: the shadowy painting of a horse with bulging eyes; the eighty-seven throw rugs overlapping each other to cover every inch of bare floor; the wedge of walled-in space (too big for a closet, too small for a bedroom) containing nothing but a baby's crib. Out back is a swath of wooden deck, beyond which is a cliff, beyond which is the churning ocean—sometimes blue, sometimes gray, depending on the light.

"Guess they're not here," Mark finally says, shrugging.

"Isn't that their Jeep out front?"

"Yeah, but they must have gone exploring. Probably taking a walk after the long drive." He carries their suitcases into the unclaimed back bedroom with a view of the trees instead of the ocean. Hannah gazes out the window, feeling either peaceful or claustrophobic, depending on the genre of story you are telling. Mark comes up behind her, wraps his arms around her waist, and then reaches down and unbuttons her jeans.

"Not now," Hannah murmurs. "They could be back any moment."

"Then we better be quick about it," Mark says, nibbling her ear, unclasping her bra. The bedroom door remains open. The pine boughs tremble in the breeze. In both stories, Hannah's bare nipples press against the cold windowpane. In both stories, Mark comes quickly. His whiskers are rough against her skin. One hand clutches a fistful of her hair. In both stories, Hannah feels a brief flicker of fear. If this is a romantic story, it is a delicious fear, and she climaxes too. If this is a scary story, it is a deeper fear that lingers after they have both pulled on their shirts and pulled up their jeans and unpacked their suitcases into the dresser drawers.

The front door opens and slams shut, followed by heavy footsteps in the hall. "Mark?" a male voice calls. Mark grins at Hannah, squeezes her hand quickly before exiting the bedroom. She follows, shy, tucking her hair behind her ears.

Mark's father and brother are also tall and broad chested, with thick hair and wide hands they wave around as they talk. They hug Mark fiercely, clapping him on the back. Mark's brother, Johnny, is two years younger, but they could easily pass as twins.

"So, this is Hannah," Mark's father says, shaking her hand. "She's even more beautiful than you described, Marky."

Johnny steps forward and envelops her in a half hug. "Hard to believe my brother hasn't scared you off yet."

"Hey now!" Mark laughs.

"Just wait," Johnny continues. "I know this guy seems sweet and charming, but we'll see what you think after spending a whole weekend with him." If this is a scary story, pause here, letting Hannah marinate in an uneasy foreboding. If this is a romantic story, Johnny winks and adds a joke about Mark's dirty socks and loud snoring, which causes Hannah to catch Mark's eye and smile because they both know she snores more than he does.

"Where's Mom?" Mark asks.

"Oh, she wasn't feeling well this morning, so she decided to stay home. She insisted we still come, though. Didn't want to ruin the trip. But we'll probably head home a day early to check on her."

Mark looks disappointed. "You too, Johnny?"

"Yeah, I'll go home with Dad. It's the only thing that makes sense." Mark's parents and Johnny live in the same town—the opposite direction from the town where Hannah and Mark live. Johnny adds, "I'm sure you two can entertain yourselves for one day without us." He shoots Hannah another wink.

If this is a romantic story, move everyone to the kitchen where they begin cooking dinner together, something simple and tasteful, and the wine flows and the laughter is easy and they rave over the tomato sauce Hannah makes for the pasta, as if she grew the tomatoes and plucked them from the vine herself. Later, as Mark and Hannah do the dishes, he discreetly squeezes her ass and kisses her neck, and she blushes, thinking of the back bedroom, the big bed waiting for them with its crisp white sheets.

But if this is a scary story, pause a few moments before the dinner preparations begin. Hannah senses tension among the father and brothers, words unspoken, secrets festering. A natural charmer of men, before this trip she was most nervous about meeting Mark's mother. But instead of relief she feels a stunning, despairing loneliness. She feels too vulnerable among these tall, strapping men, too aware of her delicate bones, her willowy limbs, her insubstantial voice. Outside the window a bird feeder hangs from the awning, and a sparrow alights on the wooden perch, pecking at the seeds. Hannah watches a blue jay chase the smaller bird away.

In the scary story, our characters do not eat pasta with tomato sauce. They eat thick steaks that Johnny and Mark sear on the grill outside, then serve rare and glistening with blood. Later, when Hannah and Mark do the dishes, she wipes pools of red off each plate with a soapy sponge and rinses fat and gristle down the garbage disposal. Mark swats her ass and kisses her neck and she thinks of the back bedroom with the large bed waiting for them, the trees standing guard outside the window, and feels trapped.

No internet access at the cabin, no cell phone service. Johnny stokes the fireplace, and everyone plays Scrabble until it's time for bed. If this is a romantic story, Mark and Hannah sleep soundly, naked and spooning. If this is a scary story, Hannah sleeps fitfully, awakened by the tree branches knocking against the window. Mark sleeps like the dead, mouth open, body still as stone.

In the morning Hannah wakes and the bed is empty. She washes her face and brushes her teeth, then wanders out to the kitchen in her robe and slippers. The men sit at the table, discussing something with stern expressions. *Arguing,* Hannah intuits. *But what about?* As soon as they see her, conversation stops and their faces reconfigure into smiles. "Hey there, sleepyhead," Mark says, reaching for her, pulling her to him. He kisses her shoulder.

Eggs and bacon and coffee for breakfast, and then everyone dresses in hiking clothes and climbs into Mark's father's Jeep. Mark's mother is an extensive researcher of activities and excursions, and this popular hiking trail topped her list. Even though she is no longer on the trip, her husband and sons feel compelled to do the hike in her honor. Hannah thinks it is sweet that the men are so devoted; or she thinks there is something a little sad, a little off, in the way they say "in her honor," as if she is dead. If you are telling a romantic story, give the trail a scenic name like Seaglass Beach or Montaña Bonita. If you are telling a scary story, name it something like Devil's Creek or Diablo Vista.

They pull into the mostly deserted parking lot and park under the trees. Johnny studies the map while Mark leads the way onto the dirt trail. Hannah follows a couple steps behind, but if this is a scary story she feels like there is a wide gulf between her and Mark. If this is a romantic story, she closes the gap and kisses his neck whenever Johnny and their father pause to study foliage along the trail. Clouds sink in the sky, threatening rain. The trail climbs from the beach into the mountains, becoming steadily rockier and steeper. They've hiked about two miles when Hannah steps onto a loose rock and rolls her ankle. If this is a scary story, she stumbles and falls, scraping her knees and palms. If this is a romantic story, she reaches out for Mark's shoulder and he turns, steadying her in his arms.

"I'm okay," Hannah insists. "But I'm ready for a break. You guys go on ahead, and I'll rest here."

"There's no way I'm leaving you alone," Mark says. Perhaps he says it sweetly while kissing her on the cheek, or perhaps there is something almost sinister in his tone. It is decided that Johnny and their father will continue the final mile to the top, while Mark and Hannah will rest and wait for them to come back down.

"We'll take pictures for you!" Johnny promises, and then they vanish around the bend. Mark and Hannah sit on a fallen log a few feet off the trail. Mark wipes his sweaty forehead and swigs from his water bottle, offering or not offering Hannah a sip, depending on what type of story you are telling.

"Sorry to ruin the hike," Hannah says.

"It's nothing," Mark says. If this is a scary story, they lapse into silence that deepens as the minutes pass.

"Are you upset?" Hannah eventually asks when she can't take it any longer.

"No, I'm fine," Mark says, in a flat and emotionless voice. Hannah looks at him and thinks, *This person is a stranger. I don't know him at all.* She flashes back to the argument she walked in on that morning in the kitchen, wondering again what the men were discussing. She looks at Mark's hands, resting on his knees, and notices their girth. *Those hands could easily strangle someone*, she thinks, then quickly pushes the thought away. Somewhere in the woods a bird calls and Hannah startles. Mark smirks. "You scared?" he teases, and she forces a laugh. That's when she asks him about the argument.

If this is a romantic story, our characters nestle close together on the moss-covered log. "Sorry to ruin the hike," Hannah says.

"You didn't ruin it. I'm just glad you're okay," Mark replies, squeezing her knee. She rests her head on his shoulder. They lapse into a comfortable silence, and Hannah thinks about the argument she walked in on that morning.

"Can I ask you a question?"

"Of course." Mark's large hand cups her knee protectively.

"What were you guys talking about earlier in the kitchen? It sounded like you were arguing. Is everything okay?"

"Yeah, it's fine," Mark says, his voice hinting at something else.

Hannah brushes his cheek with her fingertips. "You can talk to me about anything," she says.

In both the romantic and scary versions, Mark sighs before answering. "It's just—my family. My dad especially. He's super controlling, and he keeps pressuring me to do something I don't want to do. That's the whole reason he planned this trip in the first place." He runs his hand down his face. "If I don't listen to him, it'll only make things worse."

In both stories, Hannah's sprained ankle throbs. The world around her seems liquid, shimmering, and she can hear her blood in her ears. "What do you mean, make things worse?" she asks.

If this is a scary story, Mark says, "Never mind. Forget I said anything." He picks up a stick and scratches lines in the dirt. Hannah bites her lip, more unsettled than ever. It starts to drizzle.

If this is a romantic story, Mark says, "My dad might seem like a nice guy, but I've seen the way he cuts off people who cross him. Johnny was busted a couple times as a teenager for stupid drug stuff, so he wants me to confess to some shady business that's gone down. I can't go into details right now. Basically, they think I'll get a slap on the wrist or probation, not actual jail time." He picks up a stick and scratches lines in the dirt. "I wish I could just run away. Disappear."

Hannah bites her lip. "Why don't we?"

Mark looks up from the dirt, searching her face, seeing she is serious. "I love you," he says. First time he's said these words to her.

"I love you too." Tears well as he pulls her close and kisses her, and it starts to rain in full force.

They huddle under the branches, but still their clothes dampen. The trail turns to mud. Hannah thinks of the dry Jeep in the parking lot, but Mark stays put on the log, so she does too. After a few minutes, the rain throttles back to a drizzle. Johnny and their father come pounding down the trail, soaked.

"We made it!" Johnny shouts when he sees them. "Even in the rain. Gotta finish what you start, eh, Marky?" He elbows Mark in the ribs, and Mark grimaces.

They all make their way back down the trail, shoes slipping in the mud. If this is a scary story, Hannah considers sprinting off the trail into the brush. Being alone by herself in the wilderness feels somehow safer than heading back to that remote cabin with these three looming men. If this is a romantic story, Hannah brings up the rear, limping. When Mark asks, she insists she is all right, but she lets him give her a piggyback ride the final quarter mile to the parking lot.

On the drive home, the men laugh and joke, but Hannah senses palpable tension between them, a brittleness in their façade of connection.

"Mark, you should have taken Hannah back to the car sooner," his father says. "There was no need to wait for us."

"But, Dad, aren't you always saying not to abandon the family? Aren't you always going on about making sacrifices for each other?"

His father glances at Hannah in the rearview mirror. "Waiting in the rain is hardly a sacrifice," he says lightly, but his smile doesn't reach his eyes. "Now isn't the time for this conversation, Mark," he adds, a cold gruffness in his voice that Hannah has not heard before.

Back at the cabin, everyone disperses to take showers. If this is a romantic story, Hannah and Mark shower together, making love in the steam. Birds chirp sweetly outside the bathroom window. Afterward, the water still pounding down around them, Mark and Hannah whisper plans—where they'll go, what they'll do, as soon as the others leave on Sunday morning. Mark's voice echoes through Hannah's mind. *"I wish I could just run away. Disappear."* How many times has she wished the exact same thing? She kisses him fiercely. She has never felt so exhilaratingly, overwhelmingly, in love—ready to risk everything for another person.

If this is a scary tale, Hannah escapes to the bed, icing her ankle, and tells Mark he can shower first. Outside the window, the tree branches sway in the wind. Shadows dance across the wall. Mark's voice echoes through her mind. *"He keeps pressuring me to do something I don't want to do."* She wonders what the something is, and feels a strange certainty it has to do with her. *He's going to kill me,* she thinks, and almost laughs at such an absurdity. *Calm down.* She's jittery because of her surroundings. Who wouldn't be creeped out in this isolated cabin with the eerie baby's crib and proliferating throw rugs? Only two more days, and then she'll be home again, and at home things between her and Mark will return to normal. Still, she has never felt such unreasonable—yet instinctual—distrust of another person.

When Hannah steps into the living room after her shower, the men are again talking at the kitchen table, but this time they are smiling broadly—all of them, she notices, even Mark. With their hair wet and slicked back, Mark and Johnny look even more identical. It is then Hannah glimpses the suitcases, waiting in the entryway like impatient pets.

"What's going on?" she asks. "Are you leaving?"

"I got a phone call from Deb," Mark's father says. "She's feeling worse. I want to get back and make sure she's all right."

Later, Hannah will realize Mark's father must have been lying, because they don't have cell phone service at the cabin. But now, her heart pounds when she realizes she will be alone with Mark. The pounding stems either from fear or from elation, depending on what type of story you are telling. She can't read Mark's expression, his lips pressed together in an impassive line.

If this is a romantic story, Mark's father and brother leave when the first streaks of sunset spread across the sky. If this is a scary story, they leave as evening is quickening into night. Either way, Hannah and Mark stand on the front steps of the cabin, waving goodbye. Mark's arm is around Hannah's waist. Both are smiling. The Jeep revs, pulls out onto the gravel, and honks twice before disappearing down the road, out of sight. A flock of birds, sparrows or blue jays, flees the pine trees in a sudden burst, dispersing into the colorful or darkening sky.

By now your campfire burns low. By now all the s'mores have been eaten. By now your listeners are yawning, rubbing their eyes with their knuckles. It is soon time for bed.

So, it has all led to this—the ending. Make sure you get the tone exactly right. The facts are the same; tone is what matters.

Romantic story or scary story, this is how it ends: the flowers grow wild around the cabin. The trees dig their roots deeper into the soil. The blue-gray waves crash against the rocks far below. And Mark and Hannah—if those are even their names—are never heard from again.

HOW TO MAKE PAPER WHEN THE WORLD IS ENDING

T here was a path beside the ocean. She used to go for walks along it—sometimes with Jack, the family dog. The path wound along a bluff. You could look down at the beach, the children running barefoot and building sandcastles and rock sculptures, and you could look out at the deep-blue water, which seemed to stretch outward infinitely. The horizon a blurred union of ocean and sky.

• • • • • • • • •

Today is Family Day at the transfer station, which means Erin has to work on a Saturday. Rolfe is still sleeping when she leaves the apartment. She doesn't kiss him goodbye because she doesn't want to risk waking him. This early on a Saturday morning, she can't bear the sarcastic curl of his lips as he holds in some patronizing comment about her job. She grabs her daypack and her reusable mug filled with coffee and wheels her bike outside.

Early morning in mid-September, and already the asphalt of the parking lot shimmers with heat. It seems like the depths of a July afternoon—at least, what a July afternoon *used* to be like. Now, nobody ventures outside this time of year. Temperatures are at least twenty degrees warmer than average. This is the new normal. She needs to suck it up and get used to it. After all, going backwards is impossible. Their only option is to stop things here, prevent them from getting worse. No, not even *stop* things; she isn't holding out hope for that—she isn't naïve, despite what Rolfe says. Their only option is to slow down the inevitable end.

She swings a leg over her bike and pushes off toward the street. Still dozens of gas-dependent SUVs in the parking lot. She thinks about what Rolfe always says: "People don't want to change. They don't want to feel like they're sacrificing anything. It's the American way." She tries to ignore his cynical voice in her head, tries to ignore the stream of SUVs barreling past her on the road, tries to focus on her day ahead—the sustainable oasis of the transfer station, the wide-eyed innocence of the children. *"You can only do what you can do."* Her mother's words, those. But her mother isn't here anymore to say them.

· · · · · · · · ·

There was a path beside the ocean, winding along a bluff. You could look out at the deep-blue water. The horizon a blurred union of ocean and sky. She held Jack's empty leash in her hand, drumming a slow beat on her hip as she walked. Eventually, she looped back and sat on a bench, watching the surfers. She could almost see Jack out there, scampering in the sudsy surf, his black fur matted with salt water. A Labrador, he had always adored the water. "C'mon, Jack!

Let's go!" she would call after a while, and he would bound up to the hill to her, sand coating his jowls like an old man's grizzled beard.

Without Jack frolicking on the shoreline, the ocean seemed a lonelier place. She let herself cry a little, sitting on her favorite bench with Jack's leash, watching the surfers skim the waves in the slanted yellow sunlight of late afternoon.

That was the last time she walked along the path.

· · · · · · · · ·

Alice is running late again, so Erin begins setting up their paper-making booth by herself. She lugs out the tub of pulp she made yesterday, equal parts shredded office paper and water, blended together into a goopy mush. She stacks the small wooden frames in a lilting tower. Readies the pile of old newspaper. Waves good morning to Robin, her boss, who is flitting around the transfer station, making sure everything is in place. Family Day is a big event for them. "An opportunity for us to have a real presence in the community," she recalls Robin saying. She is hoping for a large turnout. There was an announcement about Family Day in the local newspaper, which is a good sign, even though no one really reads the paper anymore. Erin doesn't. Perhaps families do.

In addition to papermaking, there are booths where kids can turn plastic bottles into bird feeders, plant flowers in recycled egg cartons, and decorate aluminum cans to make pencil holders. "Perfect for back-to-school time!" Robin had exclaimed, going over the event details with the employees. Erin volunteered for the papermaking station because she's always wanted to learn how to make paper. When she was a girl, her aunt Beth had given her a fancy stationary set of handmade paper. Erin loved that paper. She loved it so much, in fact, that she could not bear to write on it. It sat in its pretty box in her desk drawer for years. Twelve thick sheets of paper, untouched. Destroyed, now. Gone. For some reason, when Erin thinks of that unused paper, it makes her so sad she swallows a lump in her throat.

It's funny—the little things that sneak up and ambush her. The tiny losses. Those can be the hardest to carry.

"Sorry, sorry, so sorry I'm late!" Alice exclaims, breathless, slamming her recycled hemp bag onto the table. Her leg bumps the tub of pulp and the water sloshes. She seems impossibly young—fresh out of college—her shiny hair pulled into a high ponytail, her wide eyes clear and alert even without coffee. No crow's-feet. No forehead wrinkles. Erin has a permanent worry wrinkle above the bridge of her nose; sometimes, standing in front of a mirror, she presses against it with the tips of her fingers, trying to smooth it out.

"What can I do to help?" Alice asks.

"I think we're pretty much set up." Erin hands her a mug. "Wanna practice before the kids come?"

· · · · · · · · ·

Here is how to make paper: dip the mug into the pulp until it is full. Pour the mushy mess onto this screen tacked inside the wooden frame. Hold the wooden frame over a plastic bucket so the water has a place to drip, so you don't soak the table. Try to spread the pulp in an even layer. There, that looks good. Now flip the frame over onto this piece of newspaper. Give it a good shake so it comes off the frame. That's normal for it to be a thick, goopy mass with a few holes. Carefully use a sponge to smooth it out, filling in the holes. Dab the soaking-wet pulp with the sponge to soak up the moisture. Wring the wet sponge out in the plastic bucket. Dab some more. As the pulp dries, apply more pressure to flatten it out. You don't want it too thick; it would take forever to dry. Keep dabbing with the sponge until you aren't soaking up much water anymore. Good job. Carefully bring your piece of paper over to the drying table, over there in the sun. It will need to dry for a day or two before you can write on it, but be sure to come pick it up from the table before you leave, okay? Enjoy the rest of Family Day!

· · · · · · · · ·

The morning passes in waves—slowly, then quickly, then slowly again. Groups of unruly children bombard the papermaking station while waiting for the bus tour to begin. The bus tour takes them around the transfer station, most notably to the landfill—"The Pit"— where the children get to walk single file across the catwalk over the ocean of garbage, squealing and pointing at the dump trucks, which are all on duty, showing off. So rare to have an appreciative audience.

The parents send their children over to the papermaking station to keep them busy for a few minutes before the bus rumbles over to take them to The Pit. Erin sends Alice into the office for more newspaper. She tries in vain to roll up a little boy's sleeves, but his jacket gets covered in paper pulp despite her best efforts. She glances over to the bus tour line, wondering if his parents will be upset. Parents are talking in little clusters, sipping the coffee that was provided in biodegradable cups, enjoying the fleeting calm while their children are occupied. Just when the tour is about to leave, the parents run over and drag their kids off to board the bus, leaving half-finished mounds of wet paper congealing on soggy pieces of newspaper.

During the quiet periods, Erin works on these abandoned paper mounds, flattening them and soaking up the excess water with sponges, then laying them out in the sun to dry. She knows most of the kids will forget to pick up their homemade paper before they leave. She knows the landfill is the main attraction, oozing rotten smells. Plus, at The Pit the kids are required by law to wear hard hats and safety vests, which they find thrilling. She knows much of the work she is doing today is useless, easily forgotten—and yet, what if it isn't? What if even one of these children is inspired to stop mindlessly throwing away paper, to instead make her own paper, to recycle and reuse more instead of wasting. Is that something? Is that enough? There's Rolfe's voice in her head again. *"Nope, we're all fucked, darlin."* She pushes away his negative apathy, plunges a mug into the goopy pulp, smiling as she helps a little girl pour the pulp onto the frame. "Here we go!" Erin says. "You're doing great!"

· · · · · · · · ·

There was a path beside the ocean where she and her mother used to go for walks sometimes, when she came home to visit. They would look down at the beach, at the children running barefoot and building sandcastles and rock sculptures. Lately, unspoken words nestled between them about children and grandchildren, fertility and adoption, the closing-in tunnel of her late thirties. Disappointment. Love. Worry. Two months ago, she had broken up with her boyfriend, the one her parents had been certain she would marry. The one she had been certain she would marry. Two months ago, her mother had driven the six hours inland to Erin's apartment, the one she used to share with the boyfriend. Her mother had swept in, scooped her out of her listless sadness, and drove her the six hours here, to her hometown, and sat beside her on this bench, holding her hand like an anchor. Looking out at the deep-blue water, seeming to stretch outward infinitely, she felt tiny tendrils of relief. The horizon a blurred union of ocean and sky, like a blessing in another language. She felt it even though she did not understand the words.

· · · · · · · · ·

Erin had not expected Rolfe to attend, but suddenly here he is, sauntering toward her. He is tall and tan and wearing another one of his lumberjack shirts. He looks out of place in the middle of the transfer station, like a cowboy in a shopping mall.

"Hey there," he says, smiling at Erin as he surveys her booth—a total mess, water and pulp splashed everywhere. "What we got goin' on here?"

"We're making paper!" a little girl shouts, sticking her hands directly into the wet pulp.

"Here, sweetie, use a mug to scoop it out," Erin says, trying to wipe the girl's hands with a towel. "Then pour the pulp into this frame, see?"

Alice rushes over and drops another armful of newspaper onto the table. They are flying through their stash; for each sheet of paper the kids make, the pulp soaks through multiple layers of newspaper. Alice immediately latches onto Rolfe. "Are you another volunteer?" she asks, sidling up and touching his arm. Erin notes the arm touching, but doesn't say anything.

"I'm happy to volunteer, yeah," Rolfe says. "But I came by to visit Erin."

"Oh," Alice says, stepping away. Her voice raises two octaves. "Erin, you didn't *tell* me you had a *boyfriend*!"

Erin just nods, helping the little girl spread the paper on the frame with the sponge. There is paper pulp in the girl's hair, on the front of her shirt—probably on her face, too.

"Actually, if you wouldn't mind . . ." Alice peels off her apron. She brought one to protect her clothing from the mess. Erin did not.

"Could you take over for me?" Alice asks Rolfe. "I hate to ask, but I just got a text from a friend of mine and it's, like, an emergency." She glances at Erin. "What? There's only, like, an hour left. Not even an hour. Besides, there's not that many kids still here."

And just like that, it's done. Erin has not even finished helping the little girl spread her paper smooth, and already Alice has passed off her apron to Rolfe and fled.

"All right," he says, winking at Erin. "How do we do this? Teach me your ways."

. . . .

One night, there was an earthquake far out in the ocean. As the people slept, a giant tsunami roared down upon the little town. It swallowed up the path beside the ocean. It swallowed up the streets and shops, the cars and the houses. It swallowed up her parents. Now there is an entirely new coastline. Her hometown is gone, wiped off the map, as if never there at all.

. . . .

Erin first met Rolfe at Whole Foods. It was one week after her family dog died and five weeks after her boyfriend moved out, and she was standing before the display of gourmet cheeses. She took the plastic-wrapped blocks into her hands, studying the colors and textures—some with fruit and nuts inside, some with names she did not recognize. She imagined she could smell their tang and sharpness through the plastic. She would smear this one on a cracker. This one, she would slice and nibble slowly, delicately. After a moment, she put them back down in the display. In her cart: spinach, carrots, apples, turkey. She was doing a special diet that month, a cleanse to expel toxins from her body. From her life. No gluten, no sugar, no dairy. No cheese.

Eventually she noticed a stocky, broad-shouldered man a couple paces away, also studying the cheese display. His hair was shaggy and he had a thick beard and wore a plaid shirt, dressed like a lumberjack for Halloween. A parody of a lumberjack, but still sexy. So different from her tall, freckled ex, he of the leather belts and the cable-knit sweaters and the responsible, trustworthy aura—except in the end it turned out she couldn't trust him at all, because he broke up with her out of the blue on a Saturday afternoon when they were supposed to be going to a potluck with friends, *his* friends, nice people she no longer talked to because deep down they were still his friends and it would be too awkward now that he had wrenched his life apart from hers.

The lumberjack, who would turn out to be Rolfe, noticed her noticing him. "Which of these cheeses, do you think?" he asked, as if they already knew each other intimately, as if they were shopping together.

"None," Erin said, mirroring his tone. "I'm not eating dairy at the moment. What about you?"

"None for me, either," he said. "I don't like cheese. I just came over here hoping to talk to you." He flashed a boyish grin, his eyes green with flecks of blue. He was just what she needed—a rebound.

A one-night stand turned into a week, two weeks, three. Her cleanse ended, and he surprised her with a platter of cheeses. It turned out she actually liked him, and not just in bed. Cynical, ironic, irreverent—so different from anyone she had dated before. She kept dating him because it was nice to choose someone from want, not just from need.

Then came the tsunami, and she couldn't fall asleep without dreaming of drowning, and she wanted him there when she startled awake in a panic at four in the morning. So he kept staying over, and then after a few months he moved in.

· · · · · · · · ·

Their family dog got cancer and her parents had to put him to sleep. The news of his death sent her back to her hometown for the weekend, to walk along the path beside the ocean and help her parents bury his ashes in the backyard under the orange tree. He used to stretch out in its shade sometimes, in the summer when it was too warm in the house. The orange tree had never produced fruit. Her father said, partly joking and partly not, that maybe now the tree would become generous. Jack was such a sweet dog, he would even be able to coax oranges from their stingy tree. It was Jack she thought of as she hugged her parents goodbye, hurriedly, anxious to get on the road and beat the traffic. Backing out of the driveway, she glanced instinctively for his doggy head at the upstairs window, but of course he was not there. She rolled down her car window, called goodbyes to her parents, that she would see them for Thanksgiving, blew a couple kisses, and drove away. She did not look back in the rearview mirror.

She did not take a mental snapshot of the house, the street, her parents waving from the front porch. It would be her final visit to her hometown—to what she still found herself thinking of as home—though of course she had no idea of this at the time. She merged onto the freeway and steered herself toward her adult life, waiting for her three hundred miles inland.

· · · · · · · · ·

"If it's any consolation, I'm sure you'll see them again before long," Rolfe had said about her parents. The initial weeks after the tsunami are blurry in Erin's mind, but she does remember him sitting down beside her on the couch, feebly patting her back as she stared, hollow eyed, out the window at the apartment parking lot. "This planet is fucked," he continued. "We've fucked it up. And there's nothing more we can do except wait for the end."

And yet, here is the same man, running after a flurry of homemade paper when it is blown off the drying table in a sudden gust of wind. Here is the same man, bending down beside a little girl, listening intently to her questions, and carefully explaining why composting is important, how it saves methane from leaking into the atmosphere, how methane is even worse than carbon dioxide at accelerating global warming. Here is the same man, helping a little boy detach the frame from the newspaper without ruining the layer of paper pulp the boy has spent a long time spreading with the sponge. As if this task is of utmost importance. As if he cares. As if this—all of this, any of this—matters.

· · · · · · · · ·

The water was a brick wall slamming into the house. The tree that never produced any oranges was ripped out of the soil like a stray weed from a garden. They had buried Jack in the soil, but now his ashes mingled with the ocean. The tides embraced him, an old friend. He had always adored the water.

· · · · · · · · ·

Rolfe describes polar bears and penguins to a boy, maybe six or seven years old. "Imagine a big giant grizzly bear, but pure white," he says, his voice thick with magic. "And little birds that stand on two feet and waddle around, like this." Erin smiles as Rolfe waddles in a small circle, imitating a penguin.

The boy laughs. "You're lying!" he says. "You're making that up!"

"Of course not! I wouldn't lie to you."

There is a slight pause. Then the boy asks, "But how do you know?"

"How do I know what?"

"About the animals."

"I saw them," Rolfe says.

"You mean they weren't extinct yet?"

Erin's heart constricts as she realizes these children learn about polar bears and penguins in the same way she learned about dinosaurs and wooly mammoths—pictures in a textbook. Fantastical creatures that never seemed quite real.

Rolfe bends so he is eye level with the boy. "I saw both polar bears and penguins in person, with my own two eyes, when I was a boy like you."

"You did?" The boy's eyes widen.

"Yep."

Suddenly the boy kicks the tub of pulp with his small sneaker. He stomps the ground. "Not fair! Not fair! I want to see them too!"

"I hear you, little man," Rolfe says, standing. "But we can't go back in time. Only forwards."

Erin pats the boy on the shoulder. "The penguins and polar bears might not be here any longer," she says. "But we can still talk about them and remember how they used to be. That's how we keep them alive—in our stories."

The boy sniffles. "But I don't want stories. I want to see them for real."

"I know," Erin says. "I know. But sometimes stories are all we have."

• • • • • • • • •

She and her father liked to walk together on the path beside the ocean. When she was maybe four or five years old, a beachside ice cream stand opened during the summer. The breeze carried the sugary scent of waffle cones baking. Her eyes lit at the array of flavors beckoning from the wide-open awning. "Please, Daddy?" she asked.

"All right," he consented. "A small scoop. Just don't tell your mom—she'd scold me for spoiling your appetite."

He handed her a scoop of vanilla topped with rainbow sprinkles on a sugar cone. She liked the crunch of the sprinkles, the way their bright colors smeared the vanilla. Her father asked if she wanted to sit on a bench and look out at the ocean as she ate her ice cream, but she shook her head no. She wanted to keep walking. She was a big girl; she could manage it.

But after only a few minutes, she stumbled on a crack in the path and yelped as she lost her grasp on the cone. It soared away from her, landing cream-first on the sandy ground. Smashed sugar cone bleeding rainbow sprinkles. Her father would not let her get another. "We have to go meet your mom for dinner," he said.

She cried, but it was not really for the loss of ice cream. It was more for the inevitability of time—the way moments could never be spun back, unraveled, relived. One moment, she was holding her ice cream cone, its taste right there on her tongue. In the next moment, her cone was ruined, a broken wreck on the pavement. She could not patch the cone back together. She could not scoop the ice cream back onto the cone. She could only go forward, never back. She could never, ever go back.

• • • • • • • • •

Finally, all the families have left. Finally, they are cleaning up. Rolfe sets a stack of newspapers down on the table. "I found these in the trash. Thought you might want them."

"Thanks. Newspapers should go in the recycling."

"These aren't just newspapers—they're paper. The paper the kids made."

Erin runs her hand over her face. She is tired. She has lugged the giant sloshing bin over to the compost pile and dumped out the leftover pulp. She has washed and dried the frames and the plastic buckets and stacked them in the office. She has swept up the hardened bits of paper pulp scattered all around the concrete patio area. She has cleaned the bathrooms, because today was supposed to be Alice's turn but Alice left, and somebody has to do it.

"Robin!" Erin calls, waving one of the still-damp papers. "Why were these in the trash?"

"Oh, they weren't in the trash. I put them in the compost bin." Robin looks unconcerned. "What? The kids didn't pick them up before they left. I told you that often happens."

The tiny losses.

"I'm sorry," Robin says, catching Erin's expression. "I didn't mean to upset you."

Sometimes for Erin, when the devastation is too much to bear, it is the tiny losses that get her.

"No, it's fine, it's just . . . the kids spent a lot of time on them, you know? They worked hard making this paper today, and I just hate thinking of it all tossed away."

"Not tossed away. It was composted," Robin says.

Erin sighs, pressing her fingers to her forehead, smoothing her worry wrinkle. "I hate to think of it just . . . decomposing."

"Let's take it home," Rolfe says. He turns to Robin. "I mean, if that's okay with you."

"Sure, whatever you like."

Rolfe helps Erin carry the abandoned paper to his car, an all-electric Volt. It occurs to her that perhaps Rolfe isn't as apathetic as he pretends. After all, if he truly believed they were all screwed, wouldn't he be driving an SUV instead of this small electric vehicle that can't even fit her bike inside?

"Are you gonna bike?" Rolfe asks. "Or do you want a ride home?"

Home. She nods. She wants to sit in the car beside him as the engine awakens without a sound and they glide like ghosts down the city streets littered with debris, just like so many streets in so many cities. *So much waste.* Perhaps theirs is a doomed city, just like her hometown. Perhaps it will be a gargantuan earthquake that destroys them, or massive wildfires, or a tornado or hurricane or snowstorm or flood. Perhaps there will be food shortages and famine, ever-rising temperatures and disease epidemics. Perhaps it will all lead to extinction, as Rolfe has predicted—a planet that has given and given and given and given, until one day it simply has nothing left to give.

He helps Erin attach her bike to the car's roof. They climb inside. He rests a hand on her knee. And she does love him, she realizes. As natural as breathing. As natural as waves crashing and receding along the shoreline. Love has crept up within her, like the temperatures slowly but steadily rising all across the earth. The knowledge engulfs her completely, undeniably.

"Thank you for coming today," Erin says. "You were a lifesaver when Alice bailed. And besides, it meant a lot to have you there. You know, supporting my work."

"I wouldn't have missed it," Rolfe says. He keeps his eyes on the road, but squeezes her knee softly. "You can only do what you can do." For once, his tone is straightforward, not a hint of sarcasm. Erin smiles. She lets her hand rest on his.

Yes, they may be doomed, but they still have today. They have the drive home. They have tonight. Hopefully, the world will not end tonight.

Tomorrow the handmade paper will be dry. She will gently pry each sheet from the newspaper and stack them carefully in a pile. She will take the pile to her desk, slip it into her drawer. And this time, she will not save the paper for some indeterminate future that may never arrive. No—she will write on it now.

· · · · · · · · ·

The horizon a blurred union of ocean and sky. The water seemed to stretch outward infinitely. You could look down at the beach, the children running barefoot and building sandcastles and rock sculptures, and you could look out at the deep-blue water. The path wound along a bluff. She used to go for walks along it—sometimes with Jack, the family dog.

There was a path beside the ocean.

FEEDING LUCIFER

The summer I turned twelve, we moved to California. At first, I was thrilled. I had spent my life surrounded by soybean fields and windmills, gray skies and muddy snow, and California was a land of palm trees and glamour. In my hometown, a small suburb outside Indianapolis, my friends' parents worked at Walmart and the Cargill plant. In California, I imagined, my friends' parents would be celebrities. Or at least paparazzi. My father's job transfer was my chance for a life upgrade.

And I was more than ready to press the "restart" button on my life. The transition to middle school had been rough—the girls who had been my friends, who just recently had been unironically playing Barbies in my Little Mermaid–wallpapered bedroom, were now wearing tight T-shirts that hugged their newly risen breasts, bra straps visible through the thin fabric like roads on a map. I wore a training bra, made even more embarrassing by the knowledge that I didn't yet need it. The shallow bra cups hung empty against my ribcage; if you pressed down, they would deflate like sad balloons. One morning, crouched in a school bathroom stall, I reached up through my baggy T-shirt and stuffed wads of toilet paper into each cup, but as the day progressed the toilet paper grew sweat-damp and itchy, and I ended up in the same bathroom stall at lunch, flushing lumps of toilet paper like giant spitballs down the toilet.

The only friend I would really miss was Lindsay, but our sadness at parting was tempered by excitement that, finally, something dramatic was happening in our lives. In the opening chords of that summer, as the damp heat swelled and gathered strength for its full debut in July, I packed the contents of my bedroom into the cardboard boxes my mother had carted home from the back lot of Payless grocery. Lindsay spent many afternoons flung across my bed, leafing through issues of *Seventeen* and occasionally proclaiming, "I can't believe you're moving! I can't believe this is happening!" I would chime in about how unfair it was, and eventually she would force herself to start crying, and then I would start crying, and finally we would hug fiercely and promise to be best friends forever and to call each other every day. Lindsay and I had been friends since kindergarten, and I knew I would miss her, but secretly I felt a shivery hunger for the newness that awaited me. I imagined a shinier, more sophisticated version of myself strolling down a breezy school hallway in California, and already in my imaginings there was a new version of Lindsay—yes, a brighter, trendier version—linking her arm through mine.

On the flight to California, my parents gave me the window seat so I could watch the collage of Midwest farms grow smaller and smaller and then disappear into a scrim of wispy clouds. I'd been on a plane once before, as a toddler when we flew to Utah for my aunt and uncle's wedding, but I had no memory of that trip. Apparently, I'd had a mild ear infection and screamed the entire flight. "Hopefully this will be a better experience," my mother said, flashing me something between a smile and a smirk as we settled into our seats. My father laughed, and my cheeks grew hot.

"Oh, sweetheart, don't be embarrassed," my mother said, making matters worse. "We're just teasing you." I jammed my headphones into my ears and turned toward the window, hating that my emotions showed so plainly across my face. Midway through the flight my stomach began to hurt. I felt like a brave, scorned character in a novel as I nibbled salt off miniature pretzels and tried to ignore the warm waves of pain below my belly button. Was this what grief felt like? Was this homesickness? I sipped Diet Coke from my small plastic cup and decided that if I had to throw up, only then would I tell my mother.

The flight seemed never-ending until suddenly we were descending into Burbank. I pressed my nose against the window. We had left Indianapolis at ten in the morning, but because of the time change it was not yet noon here. The harsh sunlight made me squint. It seemed brighter than the daylight back home. Never before had I seen so many buildings—miles and miles of buildings crammed together, vast acres of concrete and asphalt. I spotted a few squares of grass—*parks? soccer fields?*—but mostly, we were landing into a patchwork of brown and gray.

We disembarked via a staircase directly onto the tarmac, which initially seemed glamorous but actually scared me a little. I stepped carefully, gripping the railing, my stomach better but still not quite right. I was already crafting a narrative for Lindsay: *In California, everyone exits the plane like a movie star.* Later my mother would explain this wasn't a California thing, just a small-airport thing. There was a bigger airport in LA, but this smaller airport was closer to Port Hueneme, our new town. The sun beat on my shoulders;

California was a dry heat, with a breeze that swept strands of hair into my mouth. I would not tell Lindsay that the airport was much smaller than I expected, with fraying carpet and a stale smell.

In the airport bathroom, I yanked down my pants and was horrified. Had I shit myself without knowing? No, no—this was blood. What I'd been waiting for, what my mother had been asking me about for months. "Mom!" I shouted.

"Sweetheart, what's wrong? You have to undo the lock." So I did, and then my mother was wedging herself into the bathroom stall, the metal clasp of her purse banging loudly against the door. I simultaneously wanted to hide from her and cling to her, like I used to, my little-girl self hugging her legs. "I started," I mumbled, and the concern on her face shifted to understanding. Still I glimpsed traces of concern underneath, which I thought at the time related to the logistics of getting me a fresh pair of underwear. But I realize now it had more to do with the knowledge that a door had been opened, not just for me but also for her as my mother, and she could see farther through the doorway to the vast, overwhelming potential of worries and heartaches that awaited.

"It's okay," she said, stroking my hair. "Stay here. I'll be right back."

But she wasn't right back. Around me shoes shuffled, suitcases rolled, toilets flushed, sinks turned on and off, doors banged open and shut, and still my mother did not return. I wiped at the blood on my underpants with a fistful of toilet paper, only making the stain worse. By the time an unfamiliar voice called my name, I was crying.

"Madison? You in here, honey? I have something from your mom."

I raised one arm above the stall. A folded bundle slid under the door—clean underwear and a maxi pad in a bright-green wrapper. I pushed my stained underwear into the tiny trashcan labeled *Napkin Disposal*, an amenity I'd never paid much attention to before. When I emerged, I saw to my embarrassment that she was waiting for me, a lady in a security uniform with a friendly smile. She walked me to baggage claim, explaining that my mother was not allowed back into the terminal after she'd exited. "It's like that everywhere," she said. "National regulation. Where are you from?"

"Indiana."

"Yep, it's the rules in Indiana too," she said, as if I had been arguing.

"There they are." I pointed to my parents at the luggage carousel. I wanted nothing more than escape. The security woman handed me a Hershey's bar. "Midol and chocolate really help," she said. "Welcome to the club, sweetheart." She winked and disappeared back into the terminal. I was too embarrassed to say thank you; I stuffed the Hershey's bar into my backpack, where I would discover it weeks later, melted and rehardened into a deformed shape.

The farther we drove from the airport, the more distraught I began to feel. California seemed too much like Indiana. We passed strip malls with the same big-box stores and fast-food chains that beckoned from highways back home. The sky was more gray than blue, and yes, there were palm trees, but they were depressing palm trees, fronds limp and drooping. Some didn't have fronds at all, like old men gone bald.

Our new house was smaller than our house in Indiana. None of our furniture had arrived, and the empty rooms seemed lonely. We stopped at Walmart to buy air mattresses and toilet paper and a box of maxi pads. "Don't be embarrassed," my mother said. "This is something to celebrate." She put her arm around me and squeezed. I shrugged away. Being irritable kept me from thinking about how unsure and unready I felt for this new life I was standing on the cusp of.

After a dinner of takeout Chinese that we ate straight from the containers, sitting cross-legged picnic-style on the living room carpet, my parents went for a walk along the harbor. It was a chilly, fog-choked night. I stayed home, a decision I immediately regretted but was too proud to remedy by running after them. I thought about calling Lindsay, but I wanted to keep alive the illusion of my enchanted life in California. So I braided and unbraided and rebraided my hair, idly studying the ceiling in my new bedroom. My air mattress had a hole, and I could feel it gradually deflating beneath me. I placed my palms on my bra cups and pressed down; my chest was still flat.

· · · · · · · · ·

The next morning I ventured down to the beach, which is where I met Grace. My parents were busy directing the movers and beginning the tedious process of unpacking boxes, so I yelled that I was going for a walk and slipped out. I wandered up and down a few streets— Shoreline and Seashell and Beachfront. The houses were eerily uniform, the yards small rectangles of too-green grass surrounded by iron fencing; Californians, it seemed, loved fences. Eventually, I discovered a bike path that wound from our neighborhood to the sand dunes.

My first glimpse of the Pacific Ocean featured Grace, a small-silhouetted figure walking along the waves. She had a curious gait, bent slightly forward with her shoulders hunched, but that morning there was a chill in the air, so it's possible my shoulders were hunched, too. I remember thinking that she looked normal. A girl around my age. A potential friend.

California, I suddenly felt sure, would be my rescue after all. I gazed out at the steel-gray ocean stretching to the blurred horizon. Nothing in my life had prepared me for such magnificent enormity. California was not like Indiana, not at all. I took off my sandals and squeezed my toes into the cold sand. The waves rolled in and broke along the shore with an unending rhythm. Trudging barefoot toward the normal-looking girl, I thought of my ex-friends back home who stormed the school hallways in linked-armed packs of laughter and perfume, and I felt a surge of giddy confidence. Here, in my new life, I would have that too. I would belong.

When I got within shouting distance, I called out a greeting, but Grace did not turn. I jogged clumsily through the sand until I got close enough to reach out and touch her shoulder. She whirled around, her eyes frightened and a little wild, and it was then I realized she was older than me. She looked fourteen, fifteen, maybe even sixteen. My confidence faltered, like an engine stuttering, but I pressed onward. "Hi," I said, out of breath. "I'm Madison."

She was silent. The wind twisted her long, dark hair into a tangled mess of curls that she didn't bother pushing out of her eyes.

"I saw you walking and I, um, thought maybe we could be friends. I don't know anyone yet. I just moved here yesterday."

Suddenly a smile spread across her face. "I've been waiting for you," she said. Her voice was soft, almost a whisper. Perhaps the oddness of her statement should have been a clue, but I was so happy to have found a friend that I barely registered her words.

A wave rushed in and swept across our feet. The shock of cold made me jump. She asked, "Do you want to meet my friend Ezzie?"

"Sure," I said, trying to downplay my excitement. I could hardly believe my luck. My first full day in California, and I had found two friends already. A long summer of sleepovers and sunbathing and gossip unfurled before me. By the time school started, we'd be a firmly enmeshed threesome.

"This way," Grace said, taking off in the direction I'd just come. She was tall, with a fast, long-legged stride.

"What's your name?" I asked, hurrying after her.

"Oh, I'm Grace," she said, like an afterthought, as if everything between us had been established long before. We crested the sand dunes and headed back along the bike path. Grace, it turned out, lived just down the block from my new house. She walked a few paces ahead of me but kept glancing back over her shoulder, as if to make sure I was still following.

Her house was painted the same shade of gray as mine, and the inside was nearly as sparse. I glimpsed a couch, a small TV, a coffee table, and on the wall a few framed photos and an ornately carved cross. "My room's upstairs," Grace said, taking the stairs two at a time.

Her bedroom, like mine, was at the top of the stairs to the right. My first impression was claustrophobia; there was so much *stuff*. Books crammed two full bookcases and sprung up from the floor in leaning towers. Pencil drawings of dragons and fairies covered each wall in a chaotic notebook-paper collage. Stuffed animals stared, glassy eyed, from a massive pile on the bed. I crossed the room, drawn to the weak sunlight filtering in through the window.

Like mine, Grace's bedroom window looked out into the backyard. I was surprised to see they had a pool—except it was drained, nothing but a sloped concrete hole carpeted with dead leaves. There was something unsettling about a barren swimming pool in Southern California in the height of summer. I turned away from the window. "When's your friend coming?"

"Here she is," Grace said, walking towards me, cradling something alive in her hands—a small creature, a hamster maybe? I stepped back but Grace kept coming, her hands outstretched like an offering. It wasn't a hamster, I realized—it was a rat. Its long, hairless tail twitched.

"Madison, meet Esmerelda," Grace said. "Ezzie for short."

I took another half step backwards. Grace brought the rat to her chest, stroking its black fur. She bent her head close to the rat's face. "Ezzie," she said. "This is our new friend Madison."

The rat trembled, sniffing the air. Its restlessness made me anxious. I expected it to nibble at Grace's fingers, or leap out of her hands to the floor and scurry up my legs. I imagined its claws pressing into my bare skin and shuddered, wishing I had worn jeans instead of shorts.

"Do you want to hold her?" Grace asked.

"No! Um, thank you, but I've never really liked rodents." This was obviously the wrong thing to say, but Grace didn't seem offended.

"Ezzie's really sweet," Grace said. "Believe me, she never bites or scratches. I've had her since she was a little baby. She's an old girl now. Almost three, huh, Ezzie?" She reached up and set the rat on her shoulder. It immediately grew still, hanging limply from its belly, front and back legs dangling. Its black fur glistened as if oily.

"Maybe next time," I said, edging towards the bedroom door. "I just remembered, my mom wanted me to come straight home and help unpack. I'll see you later." And I fled.

Passing back through the living room, I saw something I hadn't noticed on my way in—

a giant glass cage, big enough for a dog to sleep in. It was empty. I paused, curious, but then I heard heavy footsteps coming from the kitchen, so I hurried out the front door and into the timid sunshine. The ocean breeze smelled like salt and decay.

· · · · · · · · ·

That night, I called Lindsay. "This girl is *so* weird," I told her. "You have no idea. Her best friend is a rat!" Lindsay snorted. Before long, we were both breathless with laughter. I described the strange cage in the living room and the chaos of Grace's bedroom and the creepy dredged swimming pool, embellishing details as I went along.

"You *need* to keep hanging out with her," Lindsay said. "This is, like, so entertaining. I've been dying of boredom since you left." She asked if I'd met any celebrities.

"Not yet," I said, not explaining that I lived two hours from Hollywood. I let her think that maybe tomorrow I would walk into my neighborhood Starbucks and bump into a camera crew filming a reality show.

Instead, when I went to Starbucks a week later, I bumped into Grace. She was coming out of the pet shop next door. "Madison!" she called, waving, and then she half walked, half ran over and gave me a hug. Her arms around me were surprisingly strong, and she smelled like lavender soap.

"Do you want to come over?" she asked. I was about to make

up an excuse, but then I thought of Lindsay and how I didn't have any cool stories from California yet. All I had was this strange high school girl who wanted to be my friend. So I said, "Okay."

It was another gray-skied day, and everything looked dirty. We walked mostly in silence until I asked Grace about the plastic bag she was carrying from the pet store.

"Food for Ezzie?"

"No, this is for Lucy," she said.

"Wait—you have *another* rat?"

"Lucy isn't mine; he's my dad's. And he's not a rat. He's a snake."

Inwardly, I shuddered. *Snakes!* The only thing creepier than rats, except maybe spiders. I almost asked Grace if they had spiders as pets, too, but my attention was snagged by something else. *He?* "If the snake's male, why does he have a girl's name?"

"Oh." Grace smiled, as if I were a little kid who didn't understand anything. "Lucy is a nickname. It's short for Lucifer."

Lucifer? "Like the devil?" I asked.

"Uh-huh. But there's no need to worry. My dad says that those who have been anointed by God can't die from a serpent's venom. You've been baptized, right?"

"Yeah." In Indiana we had gone sporadically to a Lutheran church down the street, mostly for special services like Christmas Eve and Easter Sunday. Then, in fifth grade, some of my friends began attending youth group at a Presbyterian Church on Wednesday evenings, so I went along too. We drank cream soda out of plastic cups and ate cookies someone's mom had baked, and Pastor Rob—the young pastor, younger than any of our parents or schoolteachers, with gelled hair and Converse sneakers—would lead Bible study. Each month was a different theme, *patience* and *charity* and *humility*, and we steadfastly worked our way through the text, reading aloud. It wasn't quite like school because Pastor Rob never called on anyone who didn't want to read; he only took volunteers. Too nervous, I never volunteered. In that room, in that church, I felt like an obvious outsider, even as I sat knee-to-knee beside my friends, with the same Preteen Devotional Companion open on my lap, wearing the same brand of jeans and the same style sweater, my hair pulled back by bobby pins instead of barrettes because barrettes had been deemed no longer cool, giggling at the same jokes and whispering together as we washed our hands in the bathroom about how *cute* Pastor Rob was, because, of course, all the girls, including me, had a crush on him.

But it seemed to me that an invisible barrier set me apart from everyone else. Perhaps because I was only pretending, acting the role I was trying so hard to get. Youth group was more about the frantic ache to belong than it was about religion. It wasn't that I didn't believe in God. But, if honest, I would have admitted that I wasn't sure I did believe in Him, either. Religion seemed tucked away high on a shelf, out of my reach. If I was uninterested, it was mostly because it did not seem particularly relevant to my life.

We walked in silence for a while, past the Mexican restaurant with three-dollar burritos and homemade tortillas, past N-V-ous Hair Salon and the frozen yogurt shop. A handful of gulls wheeled in the air. I had not yet been pooped on but made sure to always have tissues in my pocket because it could happen at any moment. You couldn't escape the seagulls. According to Grace, they flocked the campuses at lunchtime, perching on trash cans and fighting over potato chip bags. Grace was probably the type of person who made friends with the seagulls and talked to them. I pictured her standing in the middle of the quad with her arms outstretched, seagulls resting on her shoulders and wrists, one balancing atop her head, like a movie I'd seen once about a woman who raised carrier pigeons. Except seagulls were so much bigger than carrier pigeons. Heavier. Now I pictured Grace with a red face and wobbly arms, desperately trying to hold the seagulls up, and I laughed.

Grace smiled, waiting to be filled in on the joke. She was so trusting. So certain that I wanted to be her friend, too. Why? Was it because I was from the Midwest? Did I exude some hopelessly uncool vibe? I imagined this innate uncoolness, mustard yellow and dense, hovering around me like a cloud of gnats. Grace had recognized it. That was why she had linked us together so swiftly, inviting me to her house moments after we met, cheerfully introducing me to her weird pet rat. The situation made me angry. I didn't want to be linked with her. I wasn't like her.

"I thought of an inside joke," I said dismissively. "With my friends back home. You wouldn't understand."

I expected hurt to flash across Grace's face, but she seemed nonplussed. "Okay," she said, returning her gaze to the sidewalk. Her dark, tangled hair trailed behind her like a mass of seaweed, tendrils lifting in the breeze.

The street stretched before us, still four or five blocks until we turned off toward our neighborhood. "What do you have in there?" I asked, gesturing to the bag she carried from the pet store.

"Some dead mice. Food for Lucy."

I imagined them jostling about in the bag between us, their beady eyes and tiny claws and long tails, and I shuddered. In eighth grade, back home, the science classes all had to dissect mice. It was the one thing I was looking forward to missing.

"Wait! So snakes eat rodents?" I asked Grace.

She nodded.

"But what about . . . I mean . . . rats are rodents, right?"

Grace beamed. "Oh, Madison, I knew you liked Ezzie! She thought she didn't make a good impression, but I keep telling her you liked her. And now you're worrying about her. I promise, she is perfectly safe up in my room. I always close my door, and Dad keeps Lucy in his cage whenever he's not practicing. Ever since he escaped last fall, we've all been extra careful. Plus, Dad installed that extra latch on the cage."

"Oh. Um, that's good." I remembered the large cage I'd seen in the living room of Grace's house, and realized it was for the snake. *Lucifer must be a very large snake.* I didn't particularly want to go over to Grace's house anymore, but I needed more to tell Lindsay. I needed to keep her interest. She'd been talking lately about this girl Fiona Cummings, once even abruptly getting off the phone with me because Fiona was calling. I desperately needed Lindsay to stay my friend, at least through the summer. I needed someone to talk to. She was the tether to my old life. Without her, who would I have left? My parents. And, I guess, Grace. Not nearly enough.

"Madison?" Grace said, halting abruptly in the middle of the sidewalk. I stopped, too, feeling tired and annoyed. A blister was forming on my little toe from my new sandals.

"I was going to wait to ask you this," Grace said. She had a faraway look. "But since you already care so much about Esmerelda, I might as well ask you now."

Curiosity prickled my scalp. "What?"

"Would you—" She hesitated, bit her lip. "Never mind. It's too soon."

Now I *needed* to know. "What is it? Just tell me."

Grace pushed a tuft of hair behind her ear. When she spoke, her voice was nearly a whisper. "Would you be able to pet sit?"

My heart sank. *Bor-ring.* I'd been a pet sitter for lots of neighbors back home. I bent down to loosen the strap on my sandal.

"We're going on a trip," Grace continued, "for two weeks, into the wilderness. No contact with the outside world. So, we need someone responsible to care for the animals. Someone trustworthy. Ezzie gets scared of strangers, and sometimes she won't eat when I'm not around, but I can tell she likes you."

I glanced up. "Um, I don't know. How many pets do you have?"

"Just Ezzie and Lucy. And snakes don't need to eat that often. Ezzie eats twice a day, but she's really easy to feed. And she's great company. You can hang out in my room with her as much as you want." She shifted the plastic bag to her other hand. I tried not to think about the jumbled mice inside. Almost as an afterthought, she added, "Plus, my dad'll pay you."

That changed everything. Back home, I was lucky to get paid in cookies or five-dollar Dunkin Donuts gift cards. My mother said that feeding the Donaldsons' cat or taking Mrs. Hansen's golden retriever for walks, doing little favors for each other, was part of being a good neighbor. Right before we moved, I spent nearly all my allowance money on a new swimsuit.

"Sure," I told Grace. I stood up and tried to seem as capable as possible. "I can pet sit for you. No problem."

Grace looked as if she might burst into tears. She threw her arms around me. The plastic bag jostled against my hip, making me shiver. "I knew you were the one I'd been waiting for," she said.

"What?" I asked, but Grace didn't respond.

I patted her awkwardly on the back. In that moment, I didn't care that Grace was odd, that I was afraid of snakes, that Lindsay was replacing me with Fiona Cummings. Because, for the first time since I had stepped onto the tarmac at the Burbank airport, I had a plan. I would feed Grace's weird animals while her family was out of town. I would make enough money to do fun things with my new friends. And then, surely, these new friends would sweep into my life, like pieces of driftwood washing onto the shore. It was something my mother had heard on Oprah once and repeated ever since: "You must make room in your life for the future."

Grace pulled away and clapped her hands. "Ezzie will be so happy when I tell her the news!"

Come on in, future, I thought. My life has plenty of room.

• • • • • • • •

Once Grace and her family left on their trip, I ended up spending more time at their house than I had expected to. Actually, I spent a lot of time there. There's something about another person's empty house that seems less lonely than your own. My parents were at work for most of the day; at first my mother came home for lunch, but I told her she didn't need to worry about me. She worked the next town over, and it took at least twenty minutes to get from our house to her office. So, she started working through lunch and coming home an hour earlier. Before she left each morning, she would make a sandwich, seal it in plastic wrap, and put it in the fridge with a note, *Have a good day! Be safe!* Usually she drew a smiley face. They looked like fake smiles, too big, trying too hard. I promised her I wouldn't go swimming in the ocean when I was home alone. Even though I'd been taking swim lessons since I was a baby, my mother worried I would drown. "It's different than the ponds back home, Maddy," she said, her tone serious. "Riptides can pull even the strongest swimmer out to sea."

So instead, I would go over to Grace's. At first, I wandered around the empty rooms, opening cabinets and closets at random, searching—for what, I didn't know. Perhaps the most surprising thing was that I didn't find anything out of the ordinary. Grace's family had cereal and spaghetti sauce in the pantry, towels and sheets in the linen closet. No knick-knacks, no clutter. I tried the door to the master bedroom, but it was locked.

I spent most of my time in Grace's room, hanging out with Esmerelda, just as Grace had predicted. Partly because her room had the most to explore, and partly because I wanted to keep my distance from Lucifer. I dreaded feeding him.

On my fifth day of pet sitting, I found Grace's journal, a small notebook tied with pink ribbon. She kept it in her top desk drawer—not a very good hiding place. Almost as if she wanted me to find it. At least, that was what I told myself as I undid the ribbon and opened the cover. Doodles of dragons and fairies danced around the margins. Her handwriting was surprisingly neat.

Every day, I pray for a human friend. Dad says that all prayers will be answered in time. I am trying to be patient, but sometimes I get so tired of waiting. Dad says that I need to trust in . . .

I closed the journal, my gut aching with recognition. Even before we moved to California, I had tossed all my pennies into fountains and wished to be loved. Trudging down school hallways, fidgeting through youth group meetings, leaning in from the circle's edge, I had yearned for someone to notice me and understand me. I had yearned to be chosen.

In Grace's words, I could see myself. And I didn't want to be anything like Grace. *I'm not anything like Grace.*

I slid the journal back into the drawer. "Your owner is lame, Esmerelda," I said. "Praying for a human friend? It's pitiful. Not worth reading."

Esmerelda's whiskers twitched. I slid a baby carrot through the bars of her cage, and she grabbed it with her paws.

It was time, I decided, to feed Lucifer.

Grace had left careful instructions: get the bag of mice from the freezer in the garage, and thaw one mouse at a time in a bowl of warm water. "We don't cut his food up for him," she had explained. "Snakes' jaws aren't fused together at the front like humans' are." I yanked open the freezer door. It smelled bleak and sterile; frost furred the ceiling. Tugging the pet store bag out from under a package of frozen peas, I tried to decide if it would be better to use a tissue or a paper towel to extricate one of the mice—no way was I using my bare hand. I ended up taking the entire bag with me, holding one corner with the tips of my fingers.

When I flicked on the living room light, Lucifer was slithering up the side of his cage, as if trying to escape. His belly was pale, and the rest of his body was dark silver. I had no idea what type of snake he was. *Poisonous? No. Surely not.* But doubt trickled into my thoughts. What was it Grace had said? "Those who have been anointed by God can't die from a serpent's venom." Not very reassuring. Lucifer could definitely be poisonous.

Suddenly, it was too much. I looked at the door of Lucifer's cage, at the bag of mice in my hand, and knew I could not open the cage and fling a mouse inside. No way I could watch the snake unhinge his jaw and swallow the mouse whole. I left the bag of mice on the kitchen counter, escaped out the back door, and ran down the winding path to the ocean.

The waves were high, roaring up onto the sand, leaving a narrow strip of beach. I plopped down onto a dune and hugged my legs against my chest, wondering if I had ever felt so lonely. I was turning into Grace, spending all my time with a pet rat, weaving conversations from its scuttling movements and twitching whiskers. Pitiful. Boring. Scared of caged snakes and dead mice. I closed my eyes and fell back into the sand, trying to decide whether crying would make me feel better or worse.

"You're not supposed to sit there."

I blinked and sat up. A figure loomed over me, blocking the sun.

"You're supposed to stay off the sand dunes," the boy said. He looked older than me—maybe Grace's age—with shaggy blond hair, orange swim trunks, and a T-shirt with the sleeves cut off.

"Oh, um, sorry." I scrambled to stand, wiping sand from my butt. He was a head taller and smelled of sunscreen. We stood there silently, and I felt certain he was going to turn away and head back to his friends, who I could see now were looking at us from farther down the beach, making visors with their hands. But then he grinned, his eyes crinkling nearly closed, and said, "I was just messing with you. Are you new around here or something?"

I nodded. "Yeah, we just moved in down the street. I'm Madison."

"Connor," he said, reaching out to shake my hand. He had a nice smile. One of his front teeth was slightly crooked, and it made him seem carefree. As his hand closed around mine, I felt bold. I was nothing like Grace. This place was nothing like Indiana. I let my lips play into a smile and cocked my hip. "This might sound weird, but do you want to help me feed a snake?"

· · · · · · · · ·

"Whoa," Connor breathed appreciatively at the sight of Lucifer. The snake seemed even more agitated now, writhing back and forth across the cage.

"That is a huge-ass snake," his friend with the faux-hawk said. I had already forgotten both friends' names. I went to the kitchen for the package of thawed mice, exhilaration thrumming through my veins. All my senses felt sharper, as if I had slid into some higher plane of reality. The boys did rock-paper-scissors to determine who would get to feed Lucifer after I said we could only give him one mouse. The friend wearing the Sonic the Hedgehog T-shirt rifled into the package with his bare hand. I closed my eyes queasily. I didn't want to see the mouse. "Undo the cage door and toss it in," I said. "I'm going to put this back in the freezer."

"I'll come with you," a voice announced, and when I glanced back, Connor was following me.

The garage was dark. I flipped on the overhead light; Connor turned it off. I felt a shiver of fear, a new type, a not-quite-scary fear. It was a delicious fear lit with anticipation. I opened the freezer door, shoved the bag inside, shut the door. When I turned around, Connor was standing right there. His face inches from mine.

"You're pretty," he said. It was the first time a boy had ever called me that. How many hours had Lindsay and I spent in front of mirrors, poking at our faces, gleaning beauty tips from magazines, wondering what we could do to make ourselves over so boys would think we were pretty? And now, on this ordinary Thursday afternoon, when I was wearing no makeup and my hair was pulled back in a lazy ponytail, a boy had sauntered into my life and blessed me with that magic phrase. The word bloomed inside me—*pretty, pretty, pretty.*

Before I could think of a response, his mouth was on mine. I tried to tamp down my surprise. I had never been kissed before, unless you counted Timmy Malone, who pecked me on the lips in third grade on a dare. (I did not count Timmy Malone.) Kissing Connor was altogether different. His lips were warm and insistent, and his mouth tasted of peppermint gum. He pressed against me. His hands gripped my face. A tiny voice in the back of my mind urged, *Maybe this isn't a good idea. Maybe we should get back to the others.* But listening to that voice felt like trying to swim against a riptide. It was much easier to close my eyes and kiss Connor back, letting myself be pulled out to sea.

• • • • • • • • •

It felt like we had only been gone a few minutes, but when Connor and I stumbled out of the dark garage into the sunlit house, we could hear the TV blaring. His friends were sprawled on the couch. When they saw us, one raised his eyebrows and the other said, "Dude!" Whether in approval or annoyance, I couldn't tell. "I'm getting some water," I mumbled, escaping towards the kitchen. My lips felt swollen, my cheeks hot.

"How was dinner, Lucy?" I asked, pausing at the cage. With a slow, sickening lurch of my heart, I realized that something was off.

The cage was empty.

The cage door was ajar.

Lucifer was nowhere to be seen.

I yelled, "You guys, come here!" They must have heard the panic in my voice, because all three of them shuffled into the living room. "I told you to latch the cage door," I said.

"What?" Faux-hawk said.

"We did. We latched it," said Sonic the Hedgehog, but his expression was uncertain.

I gestured behind me. "Well, then the snake was able to unlatch it. Because he's not in the cage."

Connor's eyes widened. "You mean the snake escaped? It's somewhere in the house?"

I nodded. "We have to find him." And then I realized—*Esmerelda.*

I pushed past the boys and raced upstairs, taking the steps two at a time. My heart thudded like a pitiless drum in my ears. I imagined

Lucifer coiled around Ezzie's cage, preparing to strike through the bars. I prayed I had left Ezzie in her cage, where at least she would have some protection. Had I closed Grace's bedroom door?

"Hey!" a voice called from downstairs. "We gotta go! Sorry about the snake!" The front door slammed shut.

Grace's bedroom door was closed. I sighed with relief and turned the knob. The door squeaked as I pushed it open.

"Ezzie, I was so worried about you!" I strode across the room to her cage. It took me a few seconds to realize that she was motionless. Usually, she was full of shivery, twitching movement. But now her black fur was eerily still. Peering closer, I saw her eyes were like beads of glass. Lifeless.

I sank down to the floor. Logically, I knew I had not killed her. I remembered Grace saying she was old in rat years. And the bedroom door had been closed; there was no way Lucifer had gotten in. Yet, it felt like my fault. I had rushed forward into the riptide. Because of me, the devil had been let out of his cage. Maybe Ezzie had sensed the looming danger. Maybe that's why her heart stopped beating.

Eventually, I called my mother, who called animal control, who came and found Lucifer. If you looked hard enough, you could glimpse him in the empty swimming pool, slithering through dead leaves. I asked the animal control lady how he had gotten outside. She shrugged. "You must have missed an open window somewhere, hon. Even a crack these guys can slither through." She reassured me that the snake snare would not be harmful and that they would put him back in his cage.

I chose not to watch Lucifer's capture. I went inside, turned off the TV. Plodded upstairs. Curled up on Grace's bed. I felt much older than I had been that morning.

Later, I wrapped Esmerelda in some pink tissue paper, placed her gently inside a shoebox, and buried her in Grace's backyard. I wanted to wait until Grace came home but worried about leaving Esmerelda unburied for too long. I almost put her in the freezer. But

I didn't like to think of her shoved in there—frozen, beside the mice, like any other snake food.

* * * * * * * * *

Before the summer ended, Grace's family moved away. I never got to talk to her and explain. When they returned from their trip, I decided to wait a few days. That stretched into a week, then two weeks before I finally went over and rang the doorbell. I told myself I was giving things time to blow over. Part of me was scared to face Grace, and ashamed, and part of me was hoping that if I just waited long enough, the whole mess would go away. She would run up to me on the beach or outside of Starbucks, throw her thin arms around me, and say that it didn't matter, that I was still the one she had been waiting for.

But then one morning a moving van rumbled down our street and stopped in front of their house. I abandoned my cereal and ran over in my pajamas, but it was just the movers there, loading furniture. Grace and her family had already left. The movers said they weren't allowed to tell me where the truck was headed.

My parents wound up leaving, too. My mother missed the change of seasons, and my father missed the friends he had grown up with. They stayed just long enough for me to graduate high school and qualify for in-state tuition at Cal State Channel Islands. Then they moved back to Indiana. I always thought I would join them eventually. But I graduated college, found a job, met someone, and I'm still here.

Yesterday, Grace's father was on the local news. They showed a photograph of a stern-looking man with a big gray beard and round glasses. No mention of his family. All they reported was that the former pastor of a Port Hueneme church had died after refusing medical treatment for a snake bite. "Apparently, he conducted snake handling in front of his congregation," the shiny-haired news anchor said, and the co-anchor raised her perfectly arched eyebrows in surprise. *How strange!* Then they chuckled together about the next story, which featured video footage of a surfing Jack Russell terrier.

Sometimes, driving to work, I gaze out at the steely waves rolling to shore and try to remember what it was like, the first time I ever saw the ocean. The smudged horizon in the distance. The sheer enormity. I try to recapture the awe I felt, expanding inside my chest, like light flooding a darkened room. But what I remember is my first glimpse of Grace, a small figure silhouetted against the waves. I remember trudging through the sand towards her, brimming with nervous hope. Reaching out my hand to touch her shoulder. Filled with certainty, for just a moment, that all my prayers had been answered.

GOOSEPIMPLES

He isn't bothering anybody. He's just sitting in his car in the parking lot by the freshly mown soccer fields, waiting for his daughter to be done with practice. He looks at nothing in particular, just gazes out in the direction of his pony-tailed daughter and her friends, running forward and back across the field, their cheeks flushed and their toothpick legs like pinwheels in their high rainbow socks.

But he isn't really watching them, nor is he particularly aware of the pigeons squatting along the telephone wire in the distance, clumped together like old ladies gossiping, nor of the acute sky behind them, so blue it almost seems artificial. He gazes toward all of these things without really seeing them, staring vacantly into space as if deep in thought or daydreaming.

He isn't daydreaming or deep in thought, but the opposite. His mind is blank, blissfully blank, like the clear blue bowl of a sky above them, only an occasional cloud-thought skittering past, dissipating before it wakes him from peaceful emptiness.

A shadow finally rouses him, falling across his face like a summons. He glances up through the dirt-streaked windshield, expecting to see the shiny red face of his daughter, but instead he is met with the round, shapely behind of a young woman. Tight Lycra shorts grip her perfect, tan thighs. He takes in the smooth-shaven backs of her knees, her slender calves tapering down to exquisite ankles, her running shoes edged in pink trim.

Quickly he looks away, back into the blue sky, the telephone poles, the gray brick restrooms huddled amid green expanse of soccer fields. Immediately, his eyes itch to return to her. She is, after all, standing right in front of his car. Her curvaceous lower half directly eye level. Where else is he supposed to look? So he does.

She is stretching against a lamppost, still turned away from him, one leg extended far behind the other, leaning forward so her calf muscles stand out hard and tight as knots. He can't see her upper half, her face or hair or the curve of her breasts, but he can imagine. And he does. She would be one of those young girls, still in high school or just out of it, with shiny silken hair pulled back in a high ponytail, a tan glow on her cheeks. Her breasts tight swells against the fabric of her pink sports bra. She would have one of those smiles—both knowing and unknowing. Like Bridget Fitzgerald.

He never touched her. He'd been given the opportunity and wanted to, but he restrained himself. That should count for something. He merely looked. Only natural for a man to look.

He tried explaining that to his wife, but she was so busy fussing around, making a big show of packing her suitcase, that she wasn't listening. That was the last thing she told him, actually, before she took the kids and the car and left: "I don't believe a word that comes out of your sorry rotten mouth!"

After the charges were dropped, she came back. Things were strained between them for a while—four months before they had sex again—but now, six years later, the whole ordeal is all but forgotten. Or if not forgotten, never discussed—not even when they argue, which he is grateful for. It all seems so long ago.

Bridget herself would be out of college by now. She went to college out of state—Colorado, maybe, or New Mexico—and he guesses she is still out that way. He never hears from her, and he doesn't dare ask around. He hopes she is well. He hopes she is a veterinarian like she had wanted to be. He'd never met anyone who loved animals so much. Wouldn't even dissect a frog. He had given her an alternative assignment—part of the "evidence" that he gave her special treatment. It wasn't true, that part. He would have given anyone an alternative assignment. She was just the only student who had asked.

Even after the charges were dropped, he stepped down as soccer coach so as not to cause more problems. And they transferred Bridget out of his biology class and into Lynne Henderson's fifth period. Just like that, she was out of his life. He saw her once, in early spring, when walking to his car after a late afternoon of grading lab reports. She was waiting for a ride home from practice. She looked down sharply at her feet, and he walked straight on past as if he didn't see her. It pained him more than he'd imagined it would. When he got to his car, he had to sit there for a few minutes to calm his breathing.

Outside his car window, the young woman bends over at the waist, stretching her hamstrings. Lycra stretches taut.

It happened on a blustery day in late October. Bridget stayed late after practice, helping him pick up cones. She said her mom was sick with the flu and asked him for a ride home. As they headed to his car, she walked so close beside him their arms brushed. He could smell the musky sweat of her. The sun plunged behind the mountains, casting the clouds with soft pink light. "It's so beautiful," she said, flashing a knowing yet unknowing smile. "Don't you think?" He just nodded, wondering if his face betrayed his desire. He grabbed the cones from her and said, "I'll meet you in the car. It's unlocked."

When he opened the door and slid into the driver's seat, she had taken off her T-shirt and sports bra. Her breasts were pale and full in the gathering dark. The moment felt ripe with inevitability. All he had to do was reach out toward her. They were parked in the empty back lot, tucked away behind the fields. He sat there, silent, taking her in. All he had to do was reach out and touch her face, and he knew his restraint would collapse.

"Coach Blake," she said, no longer a woman at all but a girl, eyes wide and cheeks flushed, goosepimples covering her naked arms.

He turned away, ashamed. "Bridget, put your clothes back on. I'm taking you home." When he started the car, the air conditioner whooshed. He didn't reach over to turn it down because he didn't trust himself. Bridget cried quietly the entire drive, knees pulled up like a shield for her now-covered breasts. When he stopped the car in front of her house, she wiped her face and met his eyes. "I thought you liked me," she said.

"Bridget, you're my student. Nothing more."

She got out and slammed the car door. His hands shook on the steering wheel.

A week later, Principal Jones summoned, and the questioning began. It was only his word against hers. If she hadn't dropped the charges, he would have surely lost his job. And his family. Maybe even gone to jail. As it was, Principal Jones seemed relieved when he left at the end of the school year to "pursue other interests." His wife was relieved, too. She was the one who signed him up for online classes. Now he worked as a lab technician. Picked his daughter up from soccer practice and cheered her on at games. His son played ice hockey, which he didn't know much about, but he went to all those games, too. Both his kids had been too young to understand what was going on during the whole mess. They probably barely remembered it. Just thought their parents went through a rocky time. Lots of parents did. They hadn't gotten divorced, which mattered most.

The last time he saw Bridget Fitzgerald was on graduation day. Her light-blond hair glowed against the black of her robes. She was resplendent. He only saw her from a distance, one face in the wide sea of graduating faces, but during the entire ceremony she was the one he watched. When she walked across the stage to get her diploma, he applauded. He applauded for all the graduates.

Outside his windshield, the young woman finishes stretching and walks toward the other end of the parking lot. She is wearing a baggy T-shirt and her hair is light brown, hanging in one long braid down her back. He watches her walk away.

"Dad! Dad!" His daughter knocks her fist against the passenger window. The door is locked. He fumbles to unlock it. His daughter plops down into the seat. The hair around her face is darkened with sweat, and there is a streak of dirt on her forehead.

"Did you have a good practice?" he asks.

"Yeah!" she says. "I almost scored a goal during the scrimmage."

"Wow!" He notices goosepimples rising on her arms. He reaches over to turn up the heater. "Here," he says, handing her a sweatshirt from the backseat. "Put this on. You don't want to catch cold."

HOW MY PARENTS FELL IN LOVE

My mother walked out of a grocery store. She wore a red dress, her hair permed the way it looks in the photo albums. My father drove up in a car, a fast car, silver, a car that goes *vroom vroom*. He did not know her yet. She looked pretty in that red dress with ruffles at the hem. He rolled down the window, leaned out, and smiled. "Hubba, hubba!"

They fell in love and lived happily ever after.

• • • • • • • •

My mother walked out of a grocery store. She carried a plastic bag, handles stretched taut in her thin fingers. Eggs, milk, strawberries.

My father drove up in a car, *vroom vroom*. He liked my mother's red dress and her mess of dark-brown hair. He rolled down the window and said, "Hubba, hubba!"

My mother was so startled she dropped her groceries. The milk was okay, but the eggs cracked, oozing yolks onto the sidewalk. My father crouched down and helped clean up the mess. He wore dress pants and a tie, like the photos in his college yearbook.

"I'm sorry," he said.

"It's okay," she said. "It's not your fault, really."

They smiled at each other. He bought her a new carton of eggs. They fell in love and lived happily ever after.

· · · · · · · · ·

My mother walked out of the Student Union. She wore a red dress and carried a canvas book bag. My father rode up on a bicycle, glints of silver showing through the chipped paint. He wore a plain T-shirt and his hair hung down over his eyes. My mother, in a rush, distracted, digging through her bag like the nearby beach gulls dug for crabs in the sand, accidentally dropped her coin purse on the sidewalk steps. It snapped open, spilling across the cement.

My father stopped his bike with a *screeeeech*. He crouched and helped my mother collect her coins. Their skin touched as he placed pennies in her palm one by one. She smiled at him. *Hubba, hubba,* he thought.

They fell in love and lived happily ever after.

· · · · · · · · ·

My mother walked out of the rain and into the crowded apartment. She wore a red dress and her silver necklace with the star clasp. A Christmas tree beamed in the corner. People danced, laughed, tilted plastic cups against their lips.

My father noticed my mother as soon as she stepped through the doorway. Her dark hair looked darker from the rain, and beads of water trickled down her legs. He didn't know what to say, what he could ever say to her that would be enough.

So, instead, he waited. He stood by the bathroom, under the mistletoe, watching my mother and willing her to notice him.

Finally, she did, but only because she had to use the bathroom. It was occupied, so she stood in line beside my father. She, slightly drunk, spilled a bit of red wine on his shoe. He didn't mind.

"Hi," he said, glancing up at the mistletoe above them.

"Hello," my mother said. When she leaned forward to shake his hand, her necklace slipped off into a small silver puddle on the floor.

My father crouched and picked it up. Their skin touched as he placed it carefully in her palm. She smiled at him.

"Put it on for me?" she asked, pulling up her dark permed hair to reveal the back of her neck. His fingers trembled with the clasp.

"Hubba, hubba," my father found himself saying. My mother laughed.

"Look!" someone shouted. "You're under the mistletoe!"

Later, my father walked my mother back to her dormitory. They fell in love and lived happily ever after.

· · · · · · · · ·

My mother was invited to a Christmas party by a girl in her psychology class. She didn't know the girl very well, but it was a Friday night, and she had no other plans, so she went. Her dangling silver earrings flashed against her dark hair. She carried a grocery bag, handles stretched taut with the weight of the chocolate cake she had baked that morning and carefully iced with a frosting Christmas tree.

The kitchen was empty, save for three frat guys refilling their cups of eggnog, a girl arranging sugar cookies on a plate, and my father, who stood at the sink struggling in vain to wash a red wine stain from his shirt. It was hot in the kitchen, and my mother noticed a bead of sweat trickling down the back of his neck.

Suddenly, she found herself stumbling forward, tripping over something in her red high heels—a case of beer, a sack of flour, an empty cartoon of eggs? The plastic bag lurched from her grasp, and she watched the cake smash sadly against the kitchen floor.

My father turned from the sink. To him, she was just a pretty woman in a red dress.

And yet.

He hurried over and crouched to help my mother clean up the mess.

"Are you all right?" he asked.

"I'm fine," she sighed. "Just clumsy. I spent all afternoon making this cake, and now it's ruined."

"I'm sure it's still delicious," my father said, digging his hand into the dark moist cake and bringing it to his mouth. He loudly smacked his lips and grinned.

My mother laughed. My father stood, then reached down to help her up. Their skin touched. They washed cake and frosting off their hands at the sink. My father poured my mother a cup of eggnog. Their hands found each other again.

Later that night, they kissed under the mistletoe.

They fell in love.

And they lived, happily. Also angrily, naughtily, hopelessly, hungrily. Messily. Ever after. Like saints and martyrs and lovers and children. They lived, and they live. Together still.

*"*Excuse me," the man said, placing his elbows on the counter and leaning forward. "I need to make a return."

The salesclerk, a teenager with feathered bangs and rings on every finger, took her time with the shirt she was folding. The man tapped his knuckles against the counter. The clerk finished folding the shirt and gave it a little pat. She looked up and met the man's eyes.

"What can I do for you?" she asked.

"I need to make a return." The man placed a plastic bag on the counter.

"Do you have the receipt?"

"Unfortunately, no."

The salesclerk reached into the bag and pulled out a human heart. Faded to the pink of overchewed gum, it was slightly shriveled, shrunken, like leather left out for weeks in the rain and sun. It beat softly in her hand, *ka-thump, ka-thump.*

"It's my girlfriend's heart," the man explained. "Well, ex-girlfriend."

The clerk frowned. "Are you sure you got it here?" she asked. "I don't remember carrying this in our store."

"It was a while ago," the man said. "We were looking for a Christmas present for my mother. There were glass figurines where that perfume display is now." He pointed to a case by the escalators. "I told her I loved her. And she gave me her heart, right then and there." He ran his hand over his face. "I never thought I would have to return it. I didn't think I needed a receipt."

The clerk nodded. "No one ever thinks they'll need a receipt."

The man's face crumpled. The clerk busied herself with the computer. "What's your last name?" she asked after a moment.

"Weaver," the man said. He wiped his face with his sleeve and took a deep, shaky breath. The clerk continued tapping computer keys. Her rings glistened in the bright store lighting.

"Aha! Here we go," she said. "Jeremy Weaver?"

"Yes."

"And this transaction occurred . . . December 16, two years ago. You received the heart of Miss Samantha Concord."

The man's chin wobbled. He clenched his jaw to steady it. "That is correct."

The salesclerk slid the heart back into the plastic bag and placed it under the counter. "Would you like to make an exchange?"

"No . . . I mean, it's much too soon for that," the man said. "We just broke up last week."

"I can give you store credit," the salesclerk offered.

"Unless—would it be possible for me to exchange it for my own heart back?"

"Let me check," the salesclerk said, turning back to the computer. She frowned. *Tap, tap, tap.* "I'm sorry," she said after a minute. "It looks like Miss Concord has not returned the item yet."

"I figured as much—it's only been a week, like I said."

"Would you like store credit then?"

"Yeah, okay."

The salesclerk tapped the computer keys a few more times. She double-checked that the receipt printer had paper. Suddenly, she turned and touched the man's hand on the counter. "Are you sure you want to do this?" she asked. "All returns are final."

"Yes, I'm sure." The man pulled his hand away and scratched his nose. "She's moving to France for an art fellowship. Long distance is too hard."

"Why don't you go with her?"

"To France?"

"Yeah, if you love her so much. Why not?"

"It's not that simple. My whole life is here."

The clerk brushed her bangs out of her eyes. They immediately fell back into place.

"Besides," the man continued, "I don't speak French."

"You could learn. She could teach you."

"So, I uproot my life to be with her? And what if everything falls apart three months from now? What then?"

"I don't know. Come back here."

"A waste. It would be such a waste." He swallowed hard. "Sam and I agreed it's the practical thing to do."

The salesclerk nodded. They were both quiet as the printer whirred. She ripped the receipt free and smiled as she handed it to him. "Have a nice day."

The man folded the receipt twice and slid it carefully into his wallet. He turned to leave, but stopped after a couple steps.

"Excuse me!" he said.

The salesclerk looked up.

"Will you call me when she returns my heart?"

"Yes, of course."

"I'd just like to get it back," the man said. "As soon as possible."

When he had his own heart back, he would begin to heal. That was how it worked. You got your own heart back, and gradually the hurt lessened, and at some point, the receipt fell out of your wallet onto the city streets, lost among old movie tickets and gum wrappers. And then, just when your heart began to feel like yours again, you would find yourself in a department store at Christmastime with a beautiful girl, and you would swear to yourself that this time was different from all the times before; this girl was the one who would last. You would hold out the gift of your heart to her, grinning like a schoolboy, giddy with the exchange. And you wouldn't get a receipt. Because you wouldn't need it. Not this time.

Truth is, I'm not watching this damn dog because of Reginald. I'm watching it because of his sister, Reyna.

"She loves this dog, man," Reg tells me. "She'll probably come over to visit, if that's okay."

"Fine by me."

"She's prepping for a shoot in LA next week, or else she'd watch Lady for me."

"Really, it's fine."

Reginald and I were tight in high school, but then he got a scholarship to play soccer at UC Riverside. Which everyone knows is the worst UC school, but don't tell that to Reg. Now he works as an accountant for H&R Block, and you can tell he thinks he's hot shit. His apartment is in the ritzy part of Oxnard, near all the hotels, right by the ocean.

I pour a bowl of Reg's fancy cereal and milk. The guy shops at Whole Foods. I try to give him shit about it, but he just waves me off and never takes the bait. We used to pick fights with each other all the time. We became friends because he punched me after soccer practice one day in high school, accusing me of holding his jersey. Which I was, but he was holding mine, too. Parties weren't parties without us getting in some drunken argument and trying to push each other down the stairs. But that was back in high school. Doesn't seem that long ago to me, but to Reg it does.

Reyna stops by in the afternoon. She has this shiny hair that goes down to her hips, and these huge round eyes that make her look innocent, which is sexy as hell because you know she's not. The dog runs towards her, tail swishing all over the place. Reyna crouches and coos, "Oh, my baby, oh, what a good girl."

I clear my throat. "Hey, Reyna, you want something to drink or something?"

She keeps talking to the dog as if she doesn't hear me. Then she says, "Wanna take Lady to the dog park? It's just a few blocks away."

"Yeah, okay."

"She loves the dog park. Don't you love the dog park? Yes you do. Yes you do." She hands me the leash.

"Wait," I say. "Aren't you coming?"

"I'll meet you there. I need to shower first. Reggie lets me shower here because my landlord is an asshole and won't fix the shitty water pressure. I can't even get the shampoo out of my hair."

"I can wait if you—"

"Oh no, no, look at Lady. She's all excited. I'll meet you there. Just walk down this street four blocks until you get to Rosita, then make a left and you'll see it. You can't miss it, really."

"Rosita, left. Got it." I clip the leash to the dog's collar, which isn't as easy as it sounds because the little fucker is bouncing all over the place.

"Have a good shower," I murmur, which comes out creepy. Reyna gives me a smile that doesn't look like a real smile, more like she just doesn't know what else to do with her face. She waves and disappears into the bathroom, shutting the door tight behind her. *Shit.*

Meanwhile, the dog's whining and scratching at the front door, as if it's being kept hostage. I pick up the leash, open the front door, and we're off.

· · · · · · · · · ·

The dog park does not impress me. It's just some fenced-in grass and a crappy wooden ramp for dogs to walk up and down on, and a bench where owners can sit and watch. There's only one other dog here—a huge, bulldog-looking thing, galloping around in circles like a fucking horse. Its owner is a girl around my age, with light-brown hair that reminds me of those soft toffee candies my grandma used to keep in a yellow dish on her kitchen table. I sit next to her, not too close, and pretend I'm busy focusing on Reg's dog. I unclip the leash and pat it on the back.

"Go on. Go play." I watch the dog trot away, sniffing hesitantly at the grass. It takes a few little steps, stops, sniffs, then takes a few more steps. Tedious to watch dogs run around a worn patch of grass.

I lean against the bench, twisting my body ever so slightly toward the girl with the toffee hair. She's making a big show of watching her dog, pretending like she hasn't noticed me beside her.

I want to hear what her voice sounds like.

"That your dog?" I say, pointing. "That's a nice-looking dog."

"Oh, thanks, but it's not mine. I'm watching him for a friend."

"Now, that's what I call a dog. No one will mess with you if you've got a dog like that."

She scratches her ankle. "Well, I think your dog's pretty cute."

"Oh, that's not my dog. I'm watching it for a friend, too."

She looks at me warily, like she thinks I'm making fun of her.

"Seriously!" I say. "That's my friend's dog. Reginald. He's out of town, so I'm house-sitting for him. If I had a dog, I'd never pick out one like this. Now, your dog—that's a masculine fucker."

The girl smiles, her hair still half covering her eyes, like she's playing at shy.

"Have I seen you somewhere?" I ask, even though I've never seen her before in my life. "You live around here?"

"No, not really." She pauses a few seconds, and I figure that's the end of it, she's giving me the brushoff, but then she offers, "I work at Starbucks though?" Like it's a question. It kills me when girls act all shy like that.

"Naw, I wouldn't have seen you there," I say, shaking my head. "I don't like coffee. I never go to those places. But maybe you've been to Red Lobster, over on Seaward? I used to be a waiter there."

"I don't like seafood," she says, smiling wider this time, brushing the hair from her face. I smile too, feeling good, like I'm getting somewhere, when suddenly the big-ass dog runs up and jumps on her, his huge muddy paws in her lap, licking her face like there's no tomorrow.

"Bic! Down!" she says, but it's not making any difference. I grab the dog around its chest and try to pull it off her. Torso's like a block of cement. It's panting in that crazy way dogs do, its tongue hanging sideways out of its mouth.

"Thanks," the girl says, standing to brush off her jeans. "He's a handful, as you can see." She leans and clips the leash to its collar.

"You leaving already?"

"Yeah," she says. "We were here a while before you came."

"See you here tomorrow?"

"Maybe," she says, smiling once more. And then she's gone, dragged away by that enormous dog.

I wait another twenty minutes, watching Reg's dog trot and stop, sniff and piss. Reyna never shows.

• • • • • • • • •

Walking home, I start thinking about Jewell, wondering if I'll be able to get her to eat anything tomorrow. She's been one of my residents since I first started working at Seaside Manor, right after my grandma died, which was three years ago this October. My grandma lived with us in her final months, and I took care of her when Mom was at work. It wasn't a big deal, really. I'd warm up leftovers for her, soft food my mom made—vegetable soup, mashed potatoes, creamed corn. I'd help her walk to the bathroom when she needed to. I'd rub her legs to help her circulation. Easy stuff, but it made me feel good, like someone needed me. And Grandma was grateful. Sometimes she'd just reach over and squeeze my hand. She thought I was a genius because I knew how to use Wikipedia. I started looking up weird facts online so I could tell them to her. *A male emperor moth can smell a female emperor moth up to seven miles away. About 300 million cells die in your body every minute. Rubber bands last longer when refrigerated.* I could probably have told my grandma anything and she would have believed me. But I didn't ever try to bullshit her—I didn't want to. The stranger, the better, but I only told her facts.

After she died, I dreamed about her for three straight weeks. I was nervous as hell, walking into Seaside Manor to ask if they had any jobs—wondering if they would laugh in my face when I told them I'd never been to college, didn't even have my AA degree. But Martha, the manager, seemed to like me. I had a long story prepared about how I wanted experience working in the assisted-living industry. Reginald told me to use that word, *industry*, but when I started talking, what came out was all this shit about my grandma. I had to stop talking a couple times and look at the floor because I didn't want to lose it. Martha just listened until I was done and then said, "I think we can find a place for you here."

• • • • • • • • •

My first day of work, I met Jewell, room 319. It's my job to give residents their morning medications and make sure they actually take all the pills and don't dump them in the trash or hide them in tissues. When I walked into her room that first day, Jewell was watching *The Wizard of Oz* on her small TV. Her apartment was crammed with old-lady stuff—those pillows with Bible verses on them, fake flowers in glass vases, figurines of little kids in old-style clothing. A tiny lady, the size of an elementary schooler, she loves sitting in this big armchair in front of her TV, like a throne. That day, she looked at me, her eyes sharp behind her glasses, and said, "Come watch this," pointing at the screen.

I stepped closer to the TV. The witch with the bright-green skin cackled and disappeared in a puff of smoke. "Did you know," Jewell said, "that the Wicked Witch's green makeup was made out of copper, which is very flammable, and she caught on fire while filming this scene?"

"Yeah?" I said, placing her pills one by one on the tray beside her chair.

"An extra stepped in to film the second take," Jewell continued, "and then she caught on fire, too! Both of them were severely burned. Being an actor was dangerous in those days." She stared at the TV screen, acting like she didn't see her medication, though I knew she did. She had a sly way of glancing at me out of the corner of her eye, and then at her pills, and then at me, the same way Reg used to look at me in high school when he'd try to steal Cheetos from my lunch.

"And did you know," I said to her, keeping my voice real slow and steady, "that the copper makeup was so heavy that the Wicked Witch couldn't move her face to chew, and she had to eat out of a straw for twelve days?"

Jewell looked at me sharply. I smiled and handed her a glass of water.

"No, I didn't know that," she said after a moment. "How interesting." Then she placed a pill onto her tongue and took delicate sips of water until the pills were gone.

As I turned to leave, she called after me. "What's your name, young man?"

"Phil," I told her.

"Phil," she repeated. "It's nice to meet you. I'm Ermelinda Jones."

"Nice to meet you, too, Ms. Jones."

"Jewell. I let some people call me Jewell," she said, "and you're one of them, all right?"

"All right," I said. It was a small thing, but it made me feel good.

• • • • • • • • •

Reyna's left a note on the kitchen counter. *Sorry, got a phone call and had to run. See you later! Kisses to my little Lady!*

I wander over to the fridge. One beer left. The dog's slurping up water, drooling all over the place. I wish I'd gotten that girl's number. Or even her name.

The next morning, I take Lady out before work. There's a little breeze, and you can smell the salt from the ocean. My mom always says that even though we live in a shitty house, we have it better than rich people in Arizona because they don't get to smell the ocean every day. She doesn't use the word *shitty*, but I can tell it's what she's thinking. And she's right, too. It isn't even a house really, more like a condo, two small bedrooms and a bathroom where the toilet always clogs, the neighbors above us and below us always shouting. When I got a bike for my birthday the summer I turned eleven, it was stolen two days later from the bike rack outside. Nothing left but one tire chained to the bike rack. But we have the ocean. All year long, we leave the windows cracked open to feel the ocean breeze.

I pull into the back parking lot of Seaside Manor with three minutes to spare. Martha is a nice lady and doesn't care if you're a few minutes late, which is why I don't like to be late. I don't want to take advantage. Plus, I'm worried about Jewell. I can feel it worming around in my gut, this worried feeling, no matter how much I try to keep my mind on other things—like that girl from the dog park, how I'll take Lady back there when I get home tonight, how maybe she'll be there, waiting.

Since it's the Fourth of July, people are taking the day off, and I have to work a double shift. I spend the morning setting up for the barbeque they're having at noon. After I'm done folding napkins, I make my way down the third-floor hallway with my medicine cart. Mrs. Hampton complains to me about her head cold. Mr. Rodriguez and I talk baseball. Mrs. Lacey tells me about her grandchildren, who are visiting her for dinner next week. I can never keep their names straight, but I nod and smile as she chatters away. A lot of these people just want someone to talk to.

When I get to Jewell's door, I knock twice, but there's no response. I knock again, then let myself inside. Jewell's slouched in her huge-ass armchair, eyes closed. My heart pounds. I'm at her side in three long steps, kneeling beside her, touching her arm.

"Jewell?" I say, then louder: "JEWELL?"

When my grandma died, I was the only one home. It had been a normal morning. She'd eaten breakfast, oatmeal with mushed banana mixed in—I was the one who invented that—and I turned on the TV so she could watch her soaps while I did the dishes and took a shower and whatever other shit I used to do in the mornings. When I went in to see if she needed anything, no more than an hour later, she was lying there with her eyes closed, propped up on the pillows like normal—she could have been just sleeping, easy—but my throat tightened. Something about her seemed off. Later Reg asked me to describe it, but I didn't know what to say. I guess it's just something you know. When you're the only life in a room, you can feel it.

Jewell blinks her eyes open, and I step back.

"Why are you looking at me like that?" she snaps.

"Sorry," I say. I start to say more but don't know what, so instead I focus on setting out a row of pills on her tray.

"Don't you change on me, Philip," she says. "You're the only one around here who treats me like a normal human being."

I swallow. "Do you know the Beatles?"

"Of course I do," she says.

"You know that song 'Yesterday'?"

"Everyone knows that song." She picks up a pill and holds it between two fingers, looking at me.

"Did you know the original title of that song was 'Scrambled Eggs'?"

She shakes her head. "I don't believe you." She places the pill in her mouth and swallows, then the next pill, and the next.

At lunch, she refuses to eat. "I'm not hungry. That meat looks disgusting."

I mush up some ice cream in a glass and bring it to her. "Milkshake," I say. "Made special for you. If you don't eat it, you'll hurt my feelings."

She slides the glass toward her on the table and places her lips on the thick pink straw, then pulls away. "I'm the Wicked Witch," she says, grinning, and there is a spark of something in her eyes—a bit of Reyna, of the toffee-haired girl, of my grandma?—as she wraps her lips around the straw and begins to drink.

· · · · · · · · ·

When I get back to Reg's place, it's almost five thirty. He'll be back early tomorrow morning. Lady's excited to see me, wiggling and hopping around like she's dancing. She won't even hold still long enough for me to pet her head. "That's a good girl," I say, clipping the leash onto her collar. Gonna miss coming home to her. Never thought I was a dog person, but maybe I am.

There's a woman at the dog park, around my mom's age, throwing a Frisbee for a golden retriever. That's it. No toffee-haired girl, no huge horse-dog. I unclip Lady's leash and sit on the bench, looking around in a sly way that seems like I'm not looking. And that's when I see her, running toward me across the grass. She yells something, but I can't hear the words.

"What?" I say, standing.

"Have you seen him?" She runs up to me, breathing hard. Red cheeks, wide eyes. Panicky.

"Seen who?" I ask.

"Bic, my dog. The dog I'm watching, that I had with me the other day. You remember?"

"Sure I do. That is one huge fucking dog." I smile, but she doesn't smile back. She's looking behind me, her eyes jumping around. "No, I haven't seen him," I say. "Did he run off?"

"We were on our way here when some asshole let off a firecracker, and Bic got completely spooked. All of a sudden, he took off running. I wasn't holding the leash tight enough, and it flew out of my hand. I tried chasing after him, but he's way faster than me, and I lost sight of him. I don't know where he went." Looks like she's about to cry. "Julie's gonna kill me if I lost her dog. She loves that dumb dog more than anything."

"It's okay, we'll find him. I'll help you. Lady!" I whistle. Lady's ears perk up. "Lady, c'mere!" She trots over, and I clip on her leash. The toffee-haired girl is walking fast, headed towards the street, shouting Bic's name. Lady runs along beside me, but her legs are so short she can't go fast enough. I pick her up and carry her, and she doesn't squirm at all.

I catch up to the girl at a stoplight right outside the dog park. "We should split up," she says. "Cover more ground faster." She turns to cross the street, but I touch her arm.

"What's your number?" I ask. "So I can call you if I find him."

She types it into my cell phone and rushes across the street. She's almost to the other side before I realize she didn't fill in her name. I still don't know it. I call after her, but she doesn't hear me.

I set off in the other direction down Rosita Street, walking farther away from the dog park, closer to the ocean. The breeze smells of salt and faint smoke. Barbeques, fireworks. Another bang goes off nearby. Lady barks. She's shaking in my arms. I never knew fireworks made dogs so scared.

Up ahead is another row of houses; then the street opens onto the beach. I'm half running now, shouting Bic's name. I'm feeling good. Feeling right. If I were a dog off my leash, I'd head straight to the beach.

Later, I'll tell Jewell this story. How, in the middle of a gigantic family barbecue on the beach, I find that dog Bic going to town on a plate of pulled chicken. How I manage to grab his collar and yank him away, his jowls covered in barbecue sauce, Lady yapping at us from the sand. How the toffee-haired girl legit cries on the phone when I call and tell her. How my fingers cramp holding so tight onto that dog's collar, waiting for her to arrive. How her face lights up when she runs across the beach toward us, sandals clutched in one hand, sand spewing up behind her bare feet. How she throws her arms around me and Bic in a giant hug, as Lady licks our faces and tries to scramble in too. How I finally learn her name. Sarah.

But I don't know any of that yet. All I have is this new, small kernel of hope in my chest. Now, I trudge up the sand dunes, my arms aching. Lady weighs a ton for a small dog. From the beach comes laughter and shouting, the roar of the wind. I can imagine that crazy dog here, prancing around on the sand, splashing through the waves with his cement-block chest. Yes. I can picture him so clearly. Lady barks, ears pricked up. We crest the dune and gaze out onto the beach, searching for something familiar.

FROZEN WINDMILLS

The night of the snowstorm, Sandra woke disoriented in an unfamiliar bed. The room felt too warm—stuffy, suffocating. She sat up, panic tightening her chest, blinking for a few moments until her eyes began to adjust, and she came back to her life—*February, Indiana, Kevin*. This was his apartment. He slept beside her, mouth open, breathing heavily. Sandra hadn't yet slept beside him enough to know whether he was having a nightmare. *Does he always breathe like that?* She slid out of the covers, careful not to wake him, and crept out of the bedroom. Kevin's apartment was darker than her own; she held her arms straight out in front of her and felt the walls for guidance. She would go to the kitchen and make a cup of tea and sit there until the anxiety eased its grip and she could sleep again.

Crossing the living room, her bare foot smacked against something hard, and there was a sickening snap of wood. Clutching her throbbing toes tightly in her hand, she stood on one leg like a flamingo, like the stretch they did in high school when she was on the track team. It was supposed to stretch your quads. Sandra hadn't stretched her quads in months. Winters in Indiana were so brutally cold that she hadn't run, not once, not a single step since the first snowfall back in November. Trekking to the gym was too much of a hassle, and afterwards she'd have to trudge through the snow to her car, sweat freezing on her skin beneath layers of shirts and a scarf and marshmallow coat, chilling her in a clammy way like the flu.

Cursing herself, *Clumsy, clumsy,* Sandra glanced back, and there was Kevin's guitar, shipwrecked in the middle of the living room carpet like a piece of driftwood, broken.

· · · · · · · · ·

She first met Kevin a few weeks ago, at the bagel shop across the street from the office complex where he worked as an accountant, she as a paralegal. They both went to the bagel shop occasionally for lunch, but likely would have continued not noticing one another had the waitress not mistakenly switched their sandwich orders. Sandra hadn't even been aware of the mix-up. She stared blankly out the window at the gray clouds threatening snow, nearly halfway through eating Kevin's entire turkey-bacon-tomato club, when he hesitantly approached her, holding out a ham-and-swiss like an apology. "Excuse me, miss? I think this is your sandwich."

Sandra was so embarrassed she waved him off. "Keep it—it's yours," she said. He remained awkwardly standing there beside her, and she realized he wanted *his* sandwich, not hers. Her anxiety pooled with exasperation. *Really! Can't he just go ask them to make him a new one?* With a flimsy plastic butter knife, she tried cutting away the part she'd eaten, sawing futilely at the thick bagel.

"It's okay," he said finally. "I mean, can I have yours?"

"Sure," Sandra said, relieved. "It's ham and cheese."

"Sounds good." He paused, and Sandra turned back to the window, wondering if he sensed her embarrassment, or if maybe her cheeks still looked flushed from the cold outside. "Is anyone sitting here?" he asked.

"No," Sandra said, moving her purse to make more room. He sat at the stool next to her, his long legs touching the floor under the counter. Looking back on it later, she would wonder if that was the moment some part of her had recognized his resemblance to Stephen, or if that recognition had come even earlier—if some part of her had seen it at first glance, that first *"Excuse me,"* and she had internally pushed it away, chosen to pretend not to see.

• • • • • • • • •

For their first date, Kevin took Sandra to the Indianapolis Museum of Art to see a special Basquiat exhibit. The paintings reminded Sandra of graffiti art, all bright colors and bold, shaky lines. Kevin put his arm around her as they stood in front of a painting of a crazed angel, its wings protruding erratically from its tilted body. Sandra liked the weight of Kevin's arm across her shoulders. She felt like a helium balloon, and he was her tether to the earth. The angel's halo looked sharp, pointy, as if made from barbed wire.

Years ago, Stephen had taken Sandra to the zoo and first put his arm around her in front of the giraffe exhibit. When she breathed in, he smelled like laundry detergent. Even in the sticky summer heat, Sandra had liked the weight of Stephen's arm across her shoulders. She liked the way he squeezed his eyes shut when he laughed, which made evoking his laughter feel wonderful, an accomplishment. And she liked how tall he was—six foot two, a full five inches taller than she. He could put his arm around her shoulders and make her feel small beneath its heaviness, the hairs on his arm tickling the back of her neck. *I'll have to tilt my face up to kiss him,* she had thought.

Standing there in front of the Basquiat angel, Sandra tilted up her face and pressed her lips against Kevin's. When she inhaled, he smelled like the laundry detergent Stephen had used. Kevin kissed her readily, one hand against the small of her back, pressing her to him. After a moment, Sandra pulled away. They wandered through the rest of the exhibit. At the exit, a sign informed them that Basquiat was twenty-seven when he died, and that age, twenty-seven—Stephen's age—settled painfully in Sandra's gut as if she had swallowed a rock.

It was not that night but a couple nights later that Kevin told Sandra about the windmills in his hometown. They were nestled together in his bed after sleeping together for the first time. She lay with her head on his bare chest and her feet touching his, listening as he described the way the windmills stretched across the cornfields, smooth white towers with gently rotating blades.

"That sounds like science fiction," Sandra said. "Like a Ray Bradbury story."

"No, no—not like that." Kevin sat up a little, palmed Sandra's hair with his large hand. "It's kind of beautiful, actually." He told her how, in autumn, the tall stalks of corn rippled beneath the windmills like something alive, laughing. Sandra closed her eyes and tried to picture it. Everything stirred by the same gentle force. She tipped her head back and looked at Kevin's face, or what she could see of it from that angle: sharp nose, long eyelashes, swipe of stubble along his jaw. Not a Basquiat painting; more like a Picasso.

Back in high school, she had told her best friend, Diana, that she liked Stephen, really liked him, because she could lie like this with her face pressed against his sweaty chest, very close to his armpit, and not want to move.

"You should take me there," she said to Kevin. "To the windmills." For a moment Kevin didn't respond. Sandra wondered if he hadn't heard her, or if maybe she crossed some line without realizing it. Should she clarify, retract, amend? She wasn't asking him to take her home to his family; she didn't mean that. It was much too soon for that. She just wanted to see the windmills.

But then Kevin looked down at her and smiled. "When the weather clears, we'll go."

Sandra ran her fingers down his arm and softly squeezed his hand, unsure whether to believe him. Thinking maybe she had spoken too soon, maybe the windmills should be left as something he described to her, something she could dream about.

· · · · · · · · ·

She and Stephen had dated for eleven months in high school. He was her first boyfriend. Tall and lank limbed, he walked through the halls bobbing his head, as if listening to his own personal soundtrack. She thought he was unbearably sophisticated because he liked post-Impressionist art and European techno music. He could play nearly any corny pop song on the acoustic guitar, making it sound fresh, making her love it anew. For her eighteenth birthday he gave her a print of *Starry Night*, her favorite painting. He was thoughtful and self-assured, and there was a time she loved him fully, fiercely, like a treasured part of herself.

And now she had to go home for his funeral. On WebMD, a "pulmonary embolism" was explained as a blood clot forming and traveling to your lungs, causing death. Paralysis greatly increased one's risk for a pulmonary embolism, the article explained. Blood pooled when muscles were not used frequently enough.

Sandra wished she hadn't looked it up. She couldn't shake the image of Stephen gasping for breath, suffocating on his own blood.

· · · · · · · · ·

Early in the morning she jolted awake, skin clammy, stomach unsettled.

Kevin stirred. "Sandra? You okay?"

"Bad dream," she said. It had been a long time since she'd dreamt of Stephen, but it hadn't surprised her when he came strolling toward her with his familiar loping walk and wide smile. He was shirtless, his skin so translucent she could see the blue veins beneath. She could see his heart, pulsing and very red, throbbing like a wound.

She had not told Kevin about Stephen. There was no reason to— not yet. Possibly not ever. Why did he need to know? She thought of the windmills and was grateful that she had never seen them. She was not ready. Once she saw them in real life, she would lose her imaginings of what they might have been.

Kevin pulled her closer, his arm draped heavily around her waist, his breathing loud and steady against her ear. Eventually she fell asleep again. They spent the rest of the morning curled against each other under blankets. Later, Kevin made peanut butter toast and hot chocolate, and he and Sandra perched on the bedroom windowsill and ate, watching the swirling currents of snow. Mounds of white obscured the streets and heaped the boughs of the trees, more snow floating down and down. If this kept up, maybe her flight would be canceled, and the decision she had agonized over for weeks—*go or not go?*—would be determined instead by Mother Nature. Sandra thought about the windmills and imagined them spinning wildly in the icy wind. Or maybe their blades would be eerily immobile, frozen.

"What are you thinking about?" Kevin asked.

"Oh, nothing." Sandra reached for the TV remote. "Okay if I check the news?"

"Sure," Kevin said, carrying their plates and mugs to the kitchen.

Back in college, Sandra began regularly watching the news to get lost in problems bigger than her own. Gradually something shifted; the news became a source of comfort, something she leaned on to feel stable. Anything could happen, yes, but the world would keep right on going, the same as always. She preferred the local news because the evening anchorwoman had a sweetly awful perm and liked to say, "Well, isn't that nice" in the same tone of voice Sandra's mother would use.

The morning anchorwoman did not have a perm; her hair looked chemically straightened, and her smile was sharp edged, a weapon. The weatherman warned of ice storms as red letters spelling out *STORM WATCH* flashed across the top of the screen. He explained that such storms were dangerous because the ice could bring down power lines. Sandra breathed in and out, anxiety spiderwebbing outward from her chest, down her arms, settling in her stomach like heavy stones. She found Kevin in the kitchen, rinsing toast crumbs off their breakfast plates.

"What if the electricity goes out?" Sandra asked.

Kevin put his arm across her shoulders; his wrist bled water through her shirt. "Don't worry, baby, I'll keep you warm." He winked. Sandra laughed but shrank away, gazing out the window at the swirls of snow. Kevin busied himself opening kitchen cabinets. "Really, though, don't worry," he said. "I've got candles here somewhere."

"I think maybe I should leave soon," Sandra said. "Before it gets dark."

"You shouldn't go out in weather like this. Stay here tonight."

"I can't."

"Getting bored of me already?"

"No, it's not like that." Sandra crossed her arms, feeling her ribs beneath her fingers. "I have a flight to catch tomorrow. I need to pack."

"A flight? Where?"

"Home."

"As in California?"

"Yeah. Just for a couple days."

Kevin studied her, and Sandra could see the questions turning in his mind. She prepared herself to stay composed when he asked why. She would calmly say, "A memorial service. A friend of mine passed away." She would not cry. She would act like an adult and deal with it because she was an adult now, twenty-six years old, and death was something adults had to deal with.

Kevin had just one question. "Do you need someone to drive you to the airport?"

And so, Sandra stayed over again.

And that was how she found herself crouching at three in the morning in the darkness of Kevin's living room, running her thumb back and forth over the snapped neck of his acoustic guitar. She crouched there, feeling the break, the bent strings, the permanence of her misstep. Then she picked up the guitar, cradling it carefully against her body, and stashed it in the hall closet, behind a curtain of coats and umbrellas and a plastic sled, where she hoped Kevin would not find it for a while. At least not until she was safely aboard her flight. For the first time, she felt sure that she would go.

· · · · · · · · ·

Stephen had been paralyzed at a party eight years before. December 17, Robbie Zwick's house, a hazy-skied California night absent of stars. In the ensuing years, Sandra would examine and re-examine her memory of that night, trying to find the exact moment the party had veered off the path leading to normal and expected outcomes (cheap beer spilled on her shoes; a dull hangover; a coffee date with her best friend Diana the next morning to dissect every diminutive outfit and conversation) and had rerouted itself toward nightmare. Again and again, the moment that stuck in her memory was this: someone had the idea to go skinny-dipping. The moment that changed everything.

Afterward, nobody except for Sandra remembered whose idea it had been. Sandra remembered, because it had been her idea.

Robbie Zwick lived in the Keys, a ritzy neighborhood with a wide mouth that opened directly onto the driftwood-studded sand of the beach. The houses were a blank-faced assembly line of white stucco walls and terra-cotta roofs. Twin rows of palm trees arched their shaggy fronds over the clean-swept sidewalks. Robbie's house had been established as a party spot in high school. His parents, both surgeons, were often working late or out of town, leaving Robbie to fend for himself with their platinum credit card and his fake ID.

They had a six-CD stereo, an ornately tiled pool and Jacuzzi tub surrounded by a large swath of smooth wooden deck, and neighbors who never called the police to complain about the noise. Word had traveled quickly that a reunion party was going down at Robbie's the Friday before Christmas, when everyone would be home from college for winter break.

Sandra was a sophomore at Purdue. As much as she loved the independence of college life, she was happy to have a break from the cold weather, the ice scrapers and chapped hands and numb lips, the vast expanse of eerie, frozen farmland that reminded her of some post-apocalyptic landscape. She was happy to be back in her California hometown, where everyone wore T-shirts and shorts, where you could skinny-dip even in winter. A Kanye song thumped from the stereo, and a dance floor was slowly forming over by the barbeque grill, under the potted palms. Sandra bobbed her head a little to the beat, taking sips from her red plastic cup, feeling glad that she had come. *Something's going to happen.* She could feel it.

She gazed around the pool deck, enjoying the cloudy film settling over her thoughts. Stephen was taller than she remembered, and he had grown out his hair a little bit, and she wanted to flirt with him and maybe make out with him later in a dark corner of Robbie Zwick's house. She was thinking about the first time they'd had sex, in the back seat of his mom's car parked at Fisherman's Point, looking out at the ocean. Her prom dress hiked up around her ribcage. The way he groaned her name when he came, then collapsed on top of her and kissed her hair. She was thinking all of this, downing the last of her third rum and Coke, feeling Stephen's eyes on her from across the pool deck as she half listened to Siggy Taylor speculate about Josephine Clerice's nose job, the stereo blasting Justin Timberlake, her best friend Diana grinding with Matt Hayward, who had gone away to Dartmouth and come back preppy chic, which was now "in." Thinking all of this, Sandra said to no one and everyone, "Let's go skinny-dipping!" and peeled off her T-shirt in one fluid motion, as if she was born to play this role in the event, as if everything were predestined.

She thought back to that moment often in later years, trying to sponge away the guilt; it had felt fated, that moment. Because the reality was, Sandra hated pools and she hated swimming and she hated her bony hips and A-cup boobs. She had never been skinny-dipping in her life.

Then other people were taking off their clothes and running out onto the pool deck, pushing each other in. Sandra eggbeatered in the deep end, the water not as warm as she had expected, goosebumps rising on her breasts and arms. A group of boys splashed each other, and water got in her eyes. There was shouting, and laughter, and then it was as if everything narrowed, a camera lens focusing, zooming in, a beat, two beats of silence, and then screams and panic erupting from the shallow end.

A body, floating there.

Stephen's hair, newly grown out.

· · · · · · · · ·

In the morning the sky felt heavy, as if the air itself were thicker. Kevin's Jeep was a bread loaf of snow. He opened the passenger door for Sandra and cleared off the snow while she sat in the frozen leather seat, trying to think of the right words to tell him about his guitar.

She couldn't come up with anything.

They were mostly quiet on the drive to Sandra's apartment for her suitcase, and then the thirty minutes to the airport, listening to the radio broadcasters warn of icy roads. Kevin drove slowly, staring hard at the road through the blur of windshield wipers. The snow kept falling. At the airport, Sandra gave Kevin a goodbye hug and fled into the security line, digging in her purse for her wallet so as not to have to watch him walk away. He'd said he would pick her up when she returned, but Sandra felt sure he would find his guitar in the next three days, and everything would fall to nothing. She imagined Kevin bringing the broken guitar with him to the airport. He would wait for her in baggage claim, holding it by the bent neck, and when she came out with the stream of weary passengers, he would thrust the guitar at her, an accusation.

Why hadn't she woken him and told him? Why hadn't she told him this morning? She could call him, but she told herself it was the type of thing better done in person. On the plane, waiting to take off, she closed her eyes and imagined driving home with him from the airport, asking him to come inside her apartment, pressing the length of her body against his as she turned the key in the lock. "I'm so sorry," she would murmur. "I broke your guitar." Maybe he wouldn't care. Maybe they would make love sweetly, gently, the way her virgin self had imagined it would always be.

· · · · · · · · ·

In high school, Sandra had been a middle-distance runner. The half mile was her race. It was the least glamorous of all the running events, but it was the only race Sandra was decent at; the quarter mile was too fast, and the full mile was too long. So, she did the half mile, and she even won a gold medal at the county championships when she was a junior and had that one shining tremendous race when her lungs didn't flare up and her legs didn't ache, as if weights that had been tied to her ankles for years were suddenly gone. She flew around the springy rubber track like a runner in a movie, with the music crescendoing in the background and triumphant cymbals crashing as she broke the tape at the finish line. That race lasted two minutes and eighteen seconds. It was the only time in her life she felt truly good at something.

Stephen had been on the track team, too; that's how they met. He made running look effortless. He floated around the track, and at the end of the race he was all smiles and strength, jogging back to cheer on his teammates while everyone else who finished after him was doubled over, hands on knees, gasping for breath.

"When I think of Stephen, it is that memory I find myself returning to most," Sandra said at the funeral, shifting her weight in her modest black shoes with the buckles that pinched, shoes she hadn't worn since her first job interview after graduating college. She thought suddenly of the shoes she had worn to prom, a sparkly silver heel with bows at the toes, the way Stephen had tenderly slipped them off her feet that night at Fisherman's Point in the back seat of his mom's car. She swallowed, tried to steady her breathing. Ever since she'd gotten off the plane, her breathing had felt shallow, as if she could not get enough air. She leaned into the cold wooden lectern and continued into the microphone. "When I think of Stephen, I picture him just after a race, radiant, waving to us in the bleachers. That is the way I want to remember him."

What she didn't say was that at times she still felt like she was running after him, or running away from him, or maybe she was bent over on the sidelines, lungs clawing for breath, unable to keep going.

· · · · · · · · ·

Kevin picked her up from the airport. She felt relief as she walked to his familiar Jeep parked unevenly against the curb—relief that he was there waiting for her, or maybe just that her real, present-tense life was waiting for her. Kevin got out to help her load her suitcase into the back. He gave her a big hug.

"Hi," she said, hugging him back.

"I missed you," he said.

Driving home, they didn't talk much. The engine hummed loudly, and his hand brushed against her knee when he reached for the gearshift. Sandra thought he probably hadn't found his guitar yet. She leaned back in her seat and gazed out the window at the light fading from the sky and snow. Kevin passed the turnoff to her apartment, then the turnoff to his apartment, and kept driving.

Sandra sat up. "Where are you going?"

"Taking you to the windmills," Kevin said.

They drove out onto Highway 52, slicing through the silent cornfields. It was dark by the time they reached Benton County. Sandra couldn't see the windmills, only their blinking red lights warning airplanes. It was both beautiful and eerie, the sea of red dots in the blackness. Sandra felt the confession rising within her.

Kevin, I have to tell you something.

It's broken.

It's my fault.

In the moment before Sandra spoke and everything came spilling out—the memorial service, skinny-dipping, the guilt she still lugged around like a heavy suitcase—she thought of her first date with Stephen. It was early August, heat rising from the cement in thick waves, and more than once Sandra escaped to the bathroom to splash water on her face and flap her arms vigorously, worried about the sweat conquering swaths of fabric below her armpits. Stephen's armpits seemed impossibly dry. He and Sandra paused in front of the giraffe enclosure. Most of the animals were out of sight in their cages, having retreated to shady patches beneath the bushes or submerged themselves in pools of water, but the giraffes were braving the sunshine, nibbling at the leafy branches of the eucalyptus trees. One of them turned, ears twitching in the faint hint of a breeze, and that's when Sandra noticed.

"Look!" she said, pointing. "Its neck—look!"

"Whoa," Stephen said.

The giraffe's neck was crooked, L-shaped, extending straight up from its body before making two sharp turns and rising to its head. It looked like the giraffe had swallowed a boomerang.

"Do you think it hurts?" Sandra had asked.

"Probably," Stephen said. Sandra flinched inwardly at his indifferent tone; perhaps Stephen noticed because he added, his voice softened, "But maybe not. Seems like he gets along fine." And that was when Stephen first put his arm around her shoulders, squeezing her body gently against his.

Suddenly, Kevin veered the Jeep to the right. He and Sandra jostled in their seats as it bumped off the highway and onto the frozen dirt of the fields. Kevin steered toward the nearest windmill. Its red light flashed a steady rhythm—on and off, on and off. Like it was warning her to stay away.

Or maybe not. Maybe it was offering guidance, beckoning her forward.

Sandra took a deep, full breath and opened her mouth to speak.

HOW TO MAKE SPINACH-ARTICHOKE LASAGNA
THREE WEEKS AFTER YOUR BEST FRIEND'S FUNERAL

1. Preheat the oven to 375 degrees F.
2. Turn on a podcast to listen to while you're cooking, perhaps *This American Life* or *RadioLab*. Something to distract you a little, cushion the silence.

The first week after she died, you stayed up late watching *Friends* reruns, which you all used to watch together in college, and you ate nothing but saltines and store-bought cookies and fruit-flavored candy, so many Starbursts you got canker sores.

But after that first week, you woke up with a panicked need to Make a Change, Improve Yourself, Learn Something New. Now every

Sunday you drive to the grocery store and load your cart with organic produce. You have smoothies for breakfast and salads for lunch, and you slice carrots and celery and bell peppers into crayon-sized sticks, which you keep in your fridge to snack on throughout the day. You listen to podcasts as you drive around town, and as you fold the laundry, and as you cook dinner. You've learned about echolocation, WWE wrestling, Kenyan distance runners, hot-air balloon bombs from World War II, and social experimentation on Facebook.

Your Facebook profile picture is the last photo you took with her, right before she caught her train to the airport. Cheeks pressed together. Gigantic smiles.

Since she died, you've started cooking more, trying out new recipes. This is your first time making lasagna.

3. Measure one cup of cottage cheese and pour into a blender or food processor. Pulse until smooth. Pour the cheese into a large mixing bowl and set aside. No need to rinse out the blender.

4. Dice an onion, preferably a red small one.

It would be a cliché to say that she was like an onion, so many layers, and difficult to get the outer layers peeled back. It would be a cliché, but it would also be true. You always thought that becoming friends with her was making a bargain with the universe: it would take at least fifty years to get past all the barriers and know her, *truly* know her, and therefore the two of you were guaranteed at least fifty years of friendship. Becoming friends with her was a long-term investment.

There were things you didn't know about her. Secrets you figured she would reveal to you one day, when she was ready. Now you wish you had asked more. You always assumed that pressing for information would backfire, make her seal her lips tighter. But maybe. Maybe she would have answered.

Blink away the onion tears. You can't remember ever seeing her cry, which bothers you. Surely you saw her cry, at some point? Surely you comforted her, at least once?

5. Sauté the diced onion in olive oil, along with minced garlic and chopped artichoke hearts. It's okay if you use pre-minced garlic in a jar, and artichoke hearts from a can. Toss in a few handfuls of spinach too. Stir it all around. Cook for a few minutes, until the onion is translucent, and the spinach is wilted.

On *This American Life*, they are talking about "vocal fry." They explain what it is—a "croaky voice"—but you can't really hear it. Which is a good thing, because apparently vocal fry is annoying, and once you start to notice, it's hard to stop noticing.

Will there come a day when you can't remember her voice? Right now you can hear her saying certain phrases very clearly—mostly silly things, inside jokes. How she used to pretend to be angry, shouting at you for being so dang pretty and smart and amazing, that she just couldn't take it anymore. And you can picture her vividly, sitting across the small café table in the sunshine the last time you saw her alive, playfully batting her eyelashes at you, saying, "How is *ze boyfriend*?" with that teasing lilt, that French accent she would put on sometimes.

Ze boyfriend is good. He's the one you're making the lasagna for; he's coming over tonight for dinner. He was supposed to meet her this summer. The two of you were planning a trip to Paris. Still are. He just won't meet her now.

6. Pour the onion-artichoke-spinach mixture into the blender and pulse until everything is chopped fine and mixed.

You've informed *ze boyfriend* that while you are still excited about the romantic trip to Paris the two of you have been planning for months, part of you is scared to go.

Paris has always belonged to her.

When you met, she was already speaking fluent French and dreaming of becoming a fashion designer. Junior year of college, you both studied abroad—she in Paris, you a Chunnel ride away in England. You took turns visiting each other. She took you to the Eiffel Tower and the Louvre and the Sacre Cour, but what you remember most vividly are small details: walking on the cobblestones beside her, arms linked; running after her down the Metro stairs to catch a train; that tiny fondue restaurant where they inexplicably served wine in baby bottles. You remember clinking your bottles together, laughing as you put your lips on the teats. You felt so grown up, but looking back it's clear; you were still babies then.

7.   Remember that large mixing bowl from earlier, with the blended cottage cheese? Pour the onion-artichoke-spinach mixture into it. Add the rest of the cottage cheese, the normal, lumpy, non-blended kind. Mix until your arm aches.

After graduation, she moved to Paris to attend fashion school, just as she always said she would. You've been to Paris one time since, to visit her. She lived a block away from the Canal Saint-Martin. Her apartment was on the sixth floor and there was no elevator; you had to walk up a narrow spiral staircase. It made you feel so European. And she seemed so European, with her French friends and French job and chic, monochromatic clothing. That visit, she took you to off-the-beaten-path places you never would have known to look for: a ramen shop in the Japanese quarter; a mosque for mint tea; an outdoor market that you ran through in the rain.

Yet she was still herself, using big gestures when talking excitedly.

Her wide smile was the same and her expressive eyes were the same and her brightly painted fingernails were the same. And her laugh was the same.

Will you ever forget her laugh? How could you? And yet, how could you not? You're only twenty-seven; you've (hopefully) got years and years left to live. Years and years to live, without her. Years and years to forget things.

8. Get out a casserole pan, and pour a thin bed of marinara sauce in the bottom. Now time for the layering. Use those no-boil lasagna noodles; seriously, they turn out fine. If they don't quite fit, break them into pieces, like crackers. Press them down into the sauce.

When you hugged goodbye for the last time, right before she caught her train to the airport, she said, "See you soon!" like she used to in college, when "soon" literally meant *soon,* meant *in a few hours after we both get home from class,* not *in six months or maybe a year when we're in the same country again.*

It is impossible that she's not a plane ride away.

9. Scoop a layer of the spinach-artichoke mixture onto the noodles. Top with shredded mozzarella cheese. Top with more marinara sauce. Top with another layer of noodles. And repeat.

With each layer, think about something you want to tell her:

about how her brother was at the funeral and he's doing great, walking and talking, expected to make a full recovery, it's really a miracle;

about how Matt came and he looks so much older than he did in college, but he skulked around in the background just like he used to do at keg parties, and how you tried to talk to him because she would have wanted you to be nice, even though you felt extremely awkward and only lasted for a couple minutes before making an excuse and escaping to the bathroom;

about how you kept waiting for her to waltz into the funeral like a female Tom Sawyer and say, "Wait, it was all a stupid joke, it was all a big mistake! I'm here!" You had expected to feel that way. What you hadn't expected was your heels-in-the-dirt dread of the funeral coming to an end. The funeral was sad and terrible and surreal, and the priest kept mispronouncing her name, but you wanted it to keep going on and on because when it was over it would be time to say goodbye, like *really* say goodbye, forever, and you weren't ready for that.

And you want to describe the cemetery to her, how it is beautiful and peaceful, and shares the same name as the street she grew up on. Holy Cross. And you want to tell her that you can't go to Paris this summer, that you can't imagine her city without her, that it's probably best if you just cancel the trip. But you know what she would say. She would widen her eyes and fling her arms around and shout, "No, you have to go! Even more now than before, you must, you must!"

And so, you will go. You will put a love lock on the Pont de l'Archevêché bridge, for her. You imagine staring up at the Eiffel Tower, tears streaming down your face, and you must admit there is something soothing in the thought. Yes, in Paris she will feel closer than anywhere else. Maybe that will be a good thing.

10. Top the final layer of noodles with marinara sauce and shredded cheese. Don't skimp on the cheese. The best part is how it gets all golden brown and bubbly on top. Now slide the whole thing into the oven and bake for forty minutes.

It's strange that she has all the answers now. She knows the answers to those big questions you occasionally talked about in college, those answerless questions about God and faith and life and death that wound their way through your skulls, extending outward into your hazy, dim futures, the bigness scaring you sometimes so you had to turn on an episode of *Friends* to settle yourselves down, dropping back into the comforting, small daily-life questions, like whether you could pull off the high-waisted shorts trend, or a laundry list of activities that Plaid Shorts Guy might be doing that was preventing him from texting you back, or if Matt would ever stop pining and sulking around the edges of your friendship group like a wounded puppy dog.

You want to ask her if she had a split second of awareness before the bus slammed broadside into their taxi. Did she know it was the end? Or was it just another moment in a seemingly infinite string of such moments, a brother visiting a sister, heading home from dinner? One moment she was turning to ask him a question, the next moment nothing. Killed instantly means no pain, right? You want her assurance that she didn't feel any pain. You want her to hold your hand and tell you she's okay. Each night when you go to sleep, you hope you might talk to her in your dreams, but it hasn't happened yet.

11. If the lasagna burns or those no-boil noodles fail to soften, toss the whole thing into the trash and make macaroni and cheese.

On her twenty-first birthday, you made two boxes of mac and cheese before you all headed out to the bars to celebrate. You packed it into a huge plastic container and slid it into the fridge to await your return.

And when you returned hours later, she was very drunk and very hungry, just as you knew she would be. You all sat around her as she ate that cold mac and cheese straight out of the plastic container. You made her drink water. You stroked her hair. And she, The Birthday Girl, for once let you all take care of her.

"This is so good!" she said as she ate. "Thank you so much for doing this!"

"You're welcome. Glad you like it." You smiled a little to yourself, taking a mental snapshot of this night—May 4, just a couple weeks before graduation, in a messy apartment in the middle of Los Angeles, surrounded by your best friends.

How is it possible she only had five more birthdays left? How is it possible that the first time you would all reunite post-graduation would not be for a wedding or a baby shower, but for her funeral?

Just babies you were back then. There was so much you did not know.

Yet, you did know enough to recognize that it was a night you would remember. The way she sat on the carpet, legs sprawled, wearing that gorgeous navy-blue chiffon dress she had designed and sewed herself. The way she ate that macaroni and cheese out of that giant plastic container with a grateful, contented smile. You knew it would be a story you would tell and retell.

And you were right. It is.

Even more now than before, it is, it is.

REAL LOVE

The good news comes on one of those falsely beautiful late-February days—sixty degrees, sunny, the icicles melting, dripping off the eaves of every building on the block. Days like this make me anxious. The weather's just a tease, flirting with springtime before dumping a barrage of snow later in the week. I've been a Midwesterner for nearly thirty years, yet the blind California optimism still creeps into my thoughts on days like this, thinking maybe spring is here early, maybe this year it will just stay like this, warm and blue skied.

"It's on!" Sam shouts into my ear. I press down my cell phone volume. Sam never talks, only shouts. Before he started our Beatles cover band, he was a high school gym teacher. He retired and decided to pursue his teenage dream of playing the drums. "Lincoln Hall wants us!" he continues.

"Really?" I don't realize until the good news come how much I expected it to be bad news. I can't shake the feeling.

"I'll give you the details at rehearsal tonight," Sam says.

I walk over to the kitchen window, yank up the blinds. Light streams in, making me squint. "Sounds great."

"Lincoln Hall!" Sam says, adopting his Ringo accent. "We're in the big leagues now, Johnny boy!"

"See you tonight," I say, hanging up before he can try to talk to me about Bill. Sam doesn't understand that there are some problems you just can't talk through. Bottom line is, I don't trust Bill. He tries to hide it, but I can tell he wants my role in the band. He wants to stick me with George's guitar riffs while he croons "Dear Prudence" to a captivated, teary-eyed audience. A woman once approached after a show and gave me a fierce, weepy hug, thanking me for bringing John Lennon back to life for a couple hours. It was one of the nicest things anyone's ever said to me. The only problem was that Bill was packing up equipment right next to me, and he heard it, too. Ever since then, he's been gunning for my spot.

I take my coffee out to my narrow balcony, standing on the splintery wood in my socks, looking down at the morning joggers and dog walkers. I still don't know anyone's names, but I wave back to those who wave to me. It's a quiet neighborhood, one of those renovated historic districts; my apartment is the top floor of an old house that's been split up into single-bedroom units. When I first moved in, I thought it would be a temporary place, just somewhere to store my boxes of crap and catch my breath after the divorce. But it's been two years, and I'm still here. It suits me, I guess.

Puddles have gathered where last night was snow. The cold dampness of the wood seeps into my socks, but I stand for a few minutes longer, watching a group of kids laughing and jostling each other on the way to the bus stop, knit caps pushed back off foreheads, jackets unzipped and flapping. Unbidden I think of Sarah as a little girl, that bright-pink headband she loved to wear, the way she'd run to give me a hug when I got home from work—her genuine excitement to see me, as if I'd been gone weeks instead of hours. Faye used to be excited to see me, too. Or maybe that's too strong of a word, *excited*. But she was happy. Pleased. Pleased that I was home, pleased to sit down beside me on the couch after the dinner had been eaten and the dishwasher had been loaded, pleased to watch a couple hours of mindless TV side by side while the dishwasher hummed and the dog snored and Sarah talked on the phone with friends up in her room. There was a time Faye didn't hate to be in the same room.

I'm starting to feel chilled in only my sweatshirt, so I head back inside, unpeeling my socks and dropping them on the carpet just inside the doorway. I'll leave them there for days because Faye isn't here to tell me not to. Two years post-divorce, it's still the small pleasures I cling to the most.

· · · · · · · · ·

I first auditioned for the role of Paul. Truth is, Paul's always been my favorite Beatle; the songs he wrote were the ones I grew up fumbling over on the guitar—but I didn't get the role. They wanted someone who could play left handed. Sam is all about authenticity.

So, leftie Rob got to be Paul, me John, and Bill George. Originally, Sam went with a different guy for George, but that guy wasn't willing to commit to Sam's required three-nights-a-week practice regimen. "If you're not serious about this, get out now!" Sam had barked at us that first rehearsal, held in his basement that he'd converted to a music room. "This band is only for *real* musicians and *real* Beatles enthusiasts. In this band, we will not only play the Beatles, we will *become* the Beatles."

Sam is our Ringo, but he lacks much of the real Ringo's charm or looks. Sam's hair sprouts out in gray tufts, a crown around his perpetually sunburned bald spot, and his round eyes bulge from his face like an angry cartoon character. Still, he gets things done. People listen to him. We listen to him.

"John!" he says, stopping us in the middle of "Come Together." He's referring to me; he insists we call each other by our Beatle names during rehearsals and performances. "You were really flat there. That's the most important part of the song. It's all building up to that chorus. You've really got to nail it, mate."

Sam brings out the awkward middle-school student still buried inside me—eager to please, easy to shame. I nod, warmth flooding my face, blood pumping in my temples. Bill smirks at me, eyes gleaming with hope. I grit my teeth and fiddle with my guitar, pretending to retune the strings. I'm not giving up my role as John. I've been playing him for nearly three years now. When I'm performing, the border between me and John Lennon fades away. I put on my long brown wig, all-white suit, and iconic round glasses, and I don't just look like John Lennon—I *am* John Lennon. For an hour or two, I bring him back to life.

· · · · · · · · ·

John Lennon died on a Monday. I was sleeping on the ancient, moldy-cushioned couch in the basement of my college dorm in Chicago. My roommate was the type of small-town high school football captain who felt swallowed up by big-city life, so insisted on being the alpha dog of the dorm. I was the type of California loner who'd spent afternoons in high school wandering alongside the ocean, tossing driftwood into the waves. I avoided confrontation, especially the physical kind. My roommate would barge into our shoebox of a dorm room with his frat guy posse, smelling of cheap cologne and cheaper whiskey, and he wouldn't even have to kick me out. I'd leave of my own volition. There was a piano in the basement I liked to play. It was missing three keys and severely out of tune, but it was comforting. Nobody else went down to the basement except to do laundry, so I was pretty much left alone. The couch was lumpy, its insides teeming with coiled springs that made it impossible to get comfortable no matter how you arranged and rearranged your limbs, but it was something, and it was more or less mine.

That night, for the first time in weeks, I went to bed happy. I'd finally met a girl who seemed to like me, too. We'd gone for coffee, and she hadn't seemed in a hurry to leave, and she hadn't seemed embarrassed to be with me even when I sloshed coffee onto my shirt. I fell asleep with her name looping through my mind—*Faye, Faye, Faye.*

The next day, I woke with a stiff back that for once didn't bother me, and I may have even been whistling as I walked across campus to my morning class. It was there I found out about John Lennon. I thought someone was making a bad joke, but there was the newspaper being passed around—*proof.* The stark black ink of the headline left no room for hope. I beelined out of class and stumbled back to my dorm where I parked myself on the piano bench and pounded out every Beatles song I could think of, especially "Julia." I ended up playing that one over and over, like a prayer. Then I called Faye. As soon as I heard her voice, I started crying.

"You're lucky I went out with you again after that," she'd say to me years later, her tone teasing but with a serious edge. "You seemed unstable, crying to a girl you'd just met."

Even at the time, she hadn't understood why I was so devastated over John's death. "Because it's the end of something big" was the closest I could get to explaining it. "He was John Lennon. He was magic." How could I put into words what his music meant to me?

"It's sad," Faye said. "But you need to get ahold of yourself. He was a great musician, but he wasn't your friend. You didn't know him."

I probably should have known then that things between us would fall apart eventually.

· · · · · · · · ·

In the weeks leading up to our Lincoln Hall performance, the intensity of rehearsals steadily escalates. It's a routine I've become familiar with from our dozens of performances for VFW gatherings and neighborhood block parties and summer festivals. Sam's excitement at booking a show quickly disintegrates into a manic striving for perfection in every note we play, every word we sing. I try not to look at Bill, try not to be alone in the same room with him. My nerves are on edge, and I don't need Bill smirking at me, making me feel like my role as John is in jeopardy.

A week before the big show, Sam decides in a caffeine-fueled frenzy to add a new song to our set list: "Real Love," a song John wrote post-Beatles and the remaining three came together and recorded after his death.

A pit opens up in my stomach.

"We'll give the audience something unexpected!" Sam says. "A song the Beatles were never able to actually sing together. We will allow them to sing it now!"

"Real Love" was the song Faye and I danced to at our wedding. The song she whispered into my ear, promising that our love was real, yes, *real.*

"John!" Sam barks. "I want your voice to stand out more on the chorus! This is your song, mate! It's all you!"

For our wedding, Faye wove tiny purple flowers into her hair that brought out the deep blue of her eyes. As we danced in the middle of the banquet hall, our friends and family gathered and watching, my arms solid around her waist, anchoring us together, she met my eyes and whispered the words along with the song.

My voice cracks in the middle of the last note. A lump in my throat. The band stops playing; I sense everyone's eyes on me.

Yearning for Faye expands inside me like it could crack my ribcage.

"All right, everyone, let's take five," Sam says. He puts his hand to his forehead, sighing, and I know he's disappointed. I'm not John Lennon today. I'm only me.

"You doing okay?" Bill asks. I hadn't noticed him walk up beside me. His eyebrows are two thick, squirming caterpillars.

"Yeah, I'm fine."

"You seemed shaky there."

I shrug. "Just need a little water." I squeeze past him, walking up the steps from Sam's basement to his kitchen. Standing at the sink, filling a glass with tap water, I try to push Faye from my mind. I need to focus.

The day I moved out, driving to my new apartment, I'd scanned the radio for a Beatles tune, any Beatles tune, but found nothing.

· · · · · · · · ·

Faye said joining the band was my version of a midlife crisis. Maybe she was right. Turning forty makes you pause, lift your head up, look around. Take stock of things. This is what I had:

a steady paycheck from a soul-draining job as an inventory analyst at United Airlines; a roommate-wife who passed me sections of the paper across the breakfast table and pecked me on the lips goodnight, but who I hadn't had a real conversation with in months; and a teenage daughter who rolled her eyes whenever I opened my mouth and snuck twenties from my wallet to buy cigarettes. Not to mention the merciless monthly clockwork of mortgage payments, my ever-expanding potbelly, and the new ache in my left knee that seemed like some irreversible marker into the realm of the elderly. I was sagging into middle-agedness, prepped for a crisis.

And then one morning before work I popped into the coffee shop across the street from my office building and saw the audition flyer Sam had posted on the community bulletin board:

EVER DREAM OF BEING A BEATLE? NOW'S YOUR CHANCE! AUDITION FOR THE LIVERPOOL BOYS, A NEW BEATLES COVER BAND PREPARING TO PLAY THE CHICAGOLAND AREA!

I tore off a slip of paper from the bottom and stuffed it into my pocket. The rest of the day I kept reaching my hand in, feeling the wisp of paper wedged between my car keys and loose change, checking to make sure it was still there. I felt myself standing taller, lifted by the hope of something new, something different. Excitement buzzed in my chest for what felt like the first time in years.

I called Sam the next morning and auditioned for the band that weekend. I played "Rocky Raccoon" and "I Will," two of my favorite Paul songs. The guitar strings were heavy under my fingers, and my voice was shaky. When Sam held up his hand to stop, I was sure he was going to tell me thanks, but no thanks. Instead, he asked if I could play "Strawberry Fields," and before I'd even reached the second chorus, he clapped his hands loudly and said, "Yes! We've found our John!" Shaking my hand as we said goodbye, he added, "Welcome to the band. You're a natural."

· · · · · · · · ·

Everyone associates John Lennon with Yoko Ono. Hardly anyone mentions his first wife, Cynthia, the mother of his son Julian. He and Cynthia married in 1962, at the beginning of Beatlemania, and the Beatles' manager insisted they keep it a secret. The fans wanted John to be single. When word got out about Cynthia and Julian, they received death threats from desperate women claiming to be in love with John. Once, a woman kicked Cynthia in the shins and told her to stay away from him.

"I don't get why you admire John Lennon at all," Faye said to me once. "He was a bastard."

"He was brilliant!"

"Cheated on his first wife, cheated on Yoko. You better not get any ideas."

· · · · · · · · ·

I hadn't told Faye about the audition. She didn't care much for my guitar playing. In the early days of our relationship, I tried to use the guitar to woo her, sitting beside her on the lumpy, patched-over couch of my college dorm and stringing together love notes into melodies, but it didn't take me long to realize her smile was forced, pasted on. When I held forth with my secondhand guitar on my lap, her eyes quickly became glazed with boredom, staring into her own faraway thoughts as she pretended to watch my fingers on the strings. By the time we married, my guitar playing had taken on an edge of secrecy, of shame—a teenage boy's pointless hobby. I only played my guitar in odd slivers of time when Faye wasn't home, or outside, late at night, when I couldn't sleep.

The first week of rehearsals, I tried making excuses of having to work late, but Faye could tell I was lying and confronted me. "Are you seeing someone?" she asked me point-blank, cornering me as I shaved after my shower. I'd wiped off a circle of the mirror to see my face; Faye's reflection was nothing but a fogged-up shadow beside me.

"No, of course not," I said. No other excuses or plausible explanations came to mind, so I told her the truth. I expected her to be embarrassed, to laugh it off. Instead, she seemed interested.

"Why didn't you tell me earlier?" she asked. "You didn't have to hide it."

"I wanted to surprise you," I lied. "We're playing our first show in a couple weeks, at Brewski's Pub."

Faye said she would be there, and in that moment I was happy. But as the date of the show approached, a steadily worsening anxiety gripped my chest. *Just nerves,* I told myself. *Stage fright.* What frightened me most was picturing Faye out there in the audience, her dark hair twisted up into a bun, her mouth set in a thin line, watching. Judging. If she came to the show, my fingers would fumble over the chords and my voice would crack when I tried to sing.

The day of the concert, after a restless night of strumming to the crickets in our backyard grass, I asked Faye not to come. Hurt leapt from her eyes, but she didn't ask for an explanation. She never asked to come to another one of my shows.

People blame Yoko for breaking up the Beatles, but I think Yoko is a scapegoat. John and Paul weren't just fighting because of Yoko. They were fighting because John was being a pompous, self-important asshole. Because he thought he was more important, more talented, than everyone else. The Beatles broke up because John wanted them to break up.

. . . .

Since the divorce, I get most information about my daughter through Faye. Sarah's a senior in high school now, and she's gotten into a couple state schools. Faye thinks she'll end up going to a community college first, then transferring. I'm not sure what she wants to study. Faye thinks she'll end up in some vaguely creative yet also practical-sounding career, like interior design or marketing. Every other weekend Sarah's supposed to stay with me, but in the beginning, she seemed to always have an excuse for why she couldn't come: food poisoning, a birthday party sleepover, a big science project that she had all the materials for at home. She never calls it her mother's house—just home. After a while, I stopped trying.

I can't get an entire weekend with my daughter, but sometimes I swing by and take her out for lunch or ice cream. When she was little, she loved rocky road sundaes. Now she just gets a small scoop of vanilla, letting half of it melt into a sticky pool in her cup uneaten while I ask about her studies and friends and drama club, because I can't think of anything else to ask. When the silence bubbling up after Sarah's one-sentence answers becomes too unbearable, I usually end up talking about the Beatles. I watch my daughter stirring circles into her melting scoop of vanilla, no doubt counting the minutes until she is back home in her mother's house, while I ramble on helplessly about number one singles and backmasking, hoping that something I say will spark her attention, even if only for a couple minutes. It hasn't happened yet. But I keep trying.

"Hi Sarah, it's your dad," I say onto her voicemail. "Just wanted to let you know my band is playing a concert next weekend, at Lincoln Hall, in the city. I've got a ticket for you if you want to come. I'll leave it at will call."

· · · · · · · · ·

We drive into the city together for the show, our equipment piled in the back of Sam's white van. It's a Friday, and the roads are congested with traffic. The clouds press down on the horizon like a down comforter, stifling. We've been on the road for maybe ten minutes when the snow begins. Sam hunches over the wheel, knuckles clenched. One of the wipers is broken, a line of rubber dragging across the windshield, forward and back, smearing condensation around.

We arrive late to Lincoln Hall, and everything is rushed, frantic. We only have time for a brief sound check before they want to let the audience inside the theater. In the dressing room, I button up my white suit, put on my long brown wig, straighten my round glasses. I look into the mirror; John Lennon stares back at me.

Sam ushers us upstairs, and we wait behind the curtain, listening to the hum of people on the other side. Blood pounds in my ears. I look down at my wingtip shoes to avoid Bill's presence. A screech of feedback, and then the announcer's voice booms over the sound system. "Let's give a warm Chicago welcome for . . . the Liverpool Boys!"

The curtain rises. I pick up my guitar, fit its strap around me like an extension of myself, and stride onstage like I belong there. The bright lights make my eyes water. I strain to make out faces in the darkened room, searching for Sarah's smile in the crowd. I can't find her, but maybe she's out there somewhere.

Paul counts us in, *one two three four*, and then my fingers are strumming out a melody I know as intimately as my own heartbeat. I raise my lips to the microphone. The crowd is cheering my name— *"John John I love you John"*—and I know it is not me they are cheering for, it is not me they love, but when I open my mouth to sing, what comes out feels more true than anything else in this life I've made for myself, so I soak in the cheers and applause and giddy shrieks— *"sing it John"*—and let myself pretend for a little while longer that it belongs to me.

THE MAN WHO LIVES IN MY SHOWER

There is a man who lives in my shower. He was here when I moved into my condo three months ago, so I didn't have much choice in the matter. When I asked what he was doing lounging in the tub, he said, "First come, first serve." Which didn't really answer my question, but the man who lives in my shower is an enigmatic guy.

He leaves when I need to take a shower. (He's not *that* kind of man.) I don't know where he goes—the living room, maybe, or the kitchen. Perhaps he simply sits on the counter beside the bathroom sink, waiting for me to be done. But he hides from me outside the bathroom. I only see him when he's in my shower.

· · · · · · · · ·

The Realtor woman—"Call me Stace"—who sold me the condo wore maroon lipstick, smudged slightly on her top lip, and electric-yellow high heels that emphasized the drab paleness of her skin. As she led me from entryway to dining alcove to bedroom, she seemed to angrily stomp each foot, but when she turned to relate some crucial point about window lighting or square footage, her smile flared like a flashbulb. We both knew she was asking too much for the place. She spoke with the tone of the celebrity chef assuring the audience how simple it is to make triple-layer cheesecake with seedless raspberry sauce, trying to convince the audience that they, too, can spin meaning out of the chaos by baking a perfectly textured dessert. In this case, my dessert was the liberated possibility of my life if I chose to buy condo 3B.

The condo was across the street from a Greek restaurant, where I imagined trying exciting new foods and becoming friends with the owners—undoubtedly a friendly old couple who would throw in free sides of baklava or bean salad. The kitchen window looked out onto a quiet street, just a block or two away from a tree-shaded park, where I could take walks in the evenings or mornings or afternoons, if I became the type of person who takes walks. Maybe I would get a dog, and then I would have a reason to take walks. A dog would probably do me good. Some company.

"I'll take it," I told Stace. Her smile slipped for a moment into a round *O* of surprise at my abruptness. After all, we hadn't even reached the bathroom yet—"Just wait till you see the *gorgeous* tile work the previous owners put in around the tub!" But, like the celebrity chef turning back to the cameras after a commercial break, she quickly regained her composure and rebooted her smile. *Say cheese!* I was momentarily blinded by the flash, and stars still twinkled in my vision as I signed the paperwork.

· · · · · · · ·

It's been two months, and I think the man who lives in my shower is becoming more comfortable with my presence—my slippers in the doorway, my bathrobe on the hook behind the door, my face lotion and toothpaste on the bathroom counter—because lately he's started talking to me. Actually, he remarks on nearly everything I do. All from the bathroom, of course. He stays in the shower and shouts out commentary. Like this morning, as I walked past the bathroom on my way down the hall to the kitchen, he yelled something I couldn't hear.

I paused, turned. "What?"

"Where are you going?" he asked, peeking out from behind the plastic shower curtain. He thinks the plastic curtain is tacky. "A floral-print cliché" he calls it. I told him I happen to like clichés. He responded by turning on the tap, soaking his head, and shaking water all over me, which I found very childish. When I told him this, he said, "I happen to like children."

"I'm going to make breakfast," I said.

"What are you making?" he asked.

"Toast."

"What kind?"

"Peanut butter. You want some?"

"No, thank you. I'm not very hungry." He's never hungry. That's another good thing about the man who lives in my shower. He's not like my college roommate, who ate my food but then pretended not to know what I was talking about when I called her on it. There are few things worse than going to the fridge expecting to see the leftover chicken curry you'd carefully boxed up and carried home the night before, only to find the second shelf has an empty place between the milk and the mushrooms and your white takeout container is in the trash.

"To be honest," the man who lives in my shower continued, "I don't like the way you make toast."

"What? I make toast fine. How can you ruin toast?" I slipped a slice into the toaster and retraced my steps to the bathroom, standing just outside the doorway so he couldn't see me in my faded flannel pajamas.

"It's not your toast, exactly. It's your bread. Why do you freeze your bread?"

"How do you know I freeze my bread?"

"I just know," he said. "But I don't understand it. Nobody likes frozen bread."

"I freeze it so it doesn't get all moldy. I can never eat a whole loaf by myself without it growing moldy."

"Can't you just buy a smaller loaf? Or split a loaf with someone?"

"That's ridiculous. Who would I split it with? And why do you even care that I freeze my bread? It works for me."

"I hate to think of you prying frozen bread slices apart with your fingers. And then sometimes the crust gets all under your fingernails. Nobody likes that."

DING! The toaster chimed. I padded back to the kitchen.

"And besides," he shouted after me, "toast doesn't taste as good when you make it with frozen bread."

"I can't even tell," I shouted back. "I think it tastes *delicious*."

"That's only because you've gotten used to frozen bread," he said. "You forget what real toast tastes like."

· · · · · · · · ·

"Why do you freeze your bread?" Ryan asked me in the last conversation we ever had. Actually, it wasn't the last conversation. We had one more conversation, later that night, but I don't like to think about that one.

I was making a sandwich for dinner, talking to him with my earbuds in, and I complained about getting pieces of crust stuck underneath my fingernails when trying to pry two frozen slices apart.

"It gets all moldy if I don't freeze it," I explained. "I can't eat a whole loaf by myself without it getting moldy."

"That is the saddest thing I've ever heard."

"Well, I'm pretty sad without you."

"I miss you too, babe," he said. "But someday we'll have a place of our own. And we won't have to freeze the bread. I'll make you fresh-bread sandwiches."

"Promise?"

"Promise."

The next day, he hung himself from his shower rod with his necktie.

· · · · · · · · ·

It was the tie with the goldfish on it, the one I picked out for him right before he left for Detroit. I bought it because Ryan and I had a pet goldfish named Sparky. Most couples buy dogs, but Ryan had horrible allergies. I didn't really mind. I liked watching little Sparky in his glass bowl beside our tiny kitchen sink. I liked the way the sunlight came in through the window and reflected off the water, and the way he swam to the surface and darted at the flakes of food I carefully shook out for him each morning and night.

When I found out about Ryan's accident—that's the word my mind still clings to, *accident*—I thought, of course, that there must be some mistake. Ryan was happy. It was a farce, a fake, a framing.

Later, when the detail surfaced about the goldfish necktie, my stomach tightened, and something inside me congealed into recognition. Ryan left no note. But I know the goldfish necktie was meant for me.

Exactly one week later, I woke up to Sparky floating belly-up in his little glass bowl, surrounded by uneaten food flakes. I couldn't bear to flush him down the toilet, so I buried him in the tiny backyard, underneath the hydrangea bushes. The hydrangeas, with their bunches of tiny white star flowers, were what you saw when you looked out the kitchen window. I liked to think Sparky had enjoyed his view of those bushes from inside his little glass bowl.

Before the hydrangeas had lost their blooms, my life was packed into boxes and I moved into my condo. I came home from work one evening to the unmistakable sound of shower water running.

"Yoo hoo, is someone home? Excuse me? Do you have any shampoo?" a voice called from the bathroom. "I'm all out."

And that is how I met the man who lives in my shower.

· · · · · · · · ·

The man who lives in my shower is shaving his moustache. I'm glad; I'm not a fan of moustaches. It looked okay on him because he always kept it neatly trimmed. But shaving is definitely an improvement. I tell him so.

"Thanks," he says. "I think."

I watch the whiskers fall into the bathroom sink. Some drift sluggishly across the counter. "You're going to clean this up, right?" I ask.

"Of course. What kind of roommate do you think I am?" He turns to face me, half his moustache gone and the other half covered in white foam. I am about to laugh, but then I see it.

The goldfish necktie. He's wearing the goldfish necktie.

"Wait . . . you're . . . the necktie." I point.

He looks at it, holds it up between his thumb and index finger, lets it flap back down. He shrugs.

My tongue is itchy. "The necktie. Where'd you . . . where'd you get that?"

He smiles. "You gave it to me."

"That's ridiculous!" I'm shrieking now. "I never gave that to you! Where'd you find it? Huh? Where?"

He shakes his head. "I won't be here much longer, Bee. Please, let's not waste time arguing." He turns back to his half-shaved moustache. His eyes, in the mirror, flit towards mine, holding my gaze for a moment, as if to see whether I understand.

I don't.

He looks away.

I stumble to my room, shut the door, and crumple into a heap on the bed, thinking of the way he would lazily run his finger around the lip of Sparky's fish bowl when we were talking in the tiny kitchen after dinner. I'd be loading the dishwasher and watching him out of the corner of my eye, his finger lightly making circles around and around and around that fishbowl. Usually, I managed to slot the last dish into place, rinse the soapsuds off my hands, and smooth my hair flat before I calmly took his hand and led him to the bedroom. Once, though—the day he finally shaved his awful moustache—I hadn't rinsed off but one plate and a wineglass before I couldn't take it any longer. I grabbed him in front of Sparky, right there in that tiny kitchen.

Tell me, isn't that what happiness is? A shiny goldfish in its bowl, hydrangea bushes in bloom, someone to love who can't even wait to finish the dishes to love you right back?

· · · · · · · · ·

When people used to ask about my engagement, I liked to tell them that it was both the happiest and saddest day of my life. Happiest because it was the day Ryan asked me to be his wife. Saddest because in the next breath he told me he was leaving.

"Jerry chose me to go to Detroit, Bee," he said.

I blinked. "What?"

"He needs to send someone, and he thinks I'm the best candidate. He told me at work today." Ryan looked up at me, still awkwardly perched on one knee beside the bed. His hands, palms-up on the bedspread, seemed lonely without the satin ring box cradled in them.

"When?" I asked.

"Three weeks."

"Wow. That's soon."

"I know—I know it is. But listen, Bee, it's only for a year. Just until you finish school. Then you can come out and join me."

"In Detroit?"

"Yeah, or, you know, wherever they transfer me after that. You know how versatile sales is. Branches close and other branches open. They send you somewhere new. But that doesn't matter. Really, Bee. Because we'll be together. Right? Look at me."

I looked into Ryan's earnest hazel eyes, at the tiny mole above his left eyebrow and the crooked part in his floppy dark hair, and the tears that had been welling up in my eyes leaked free, blurring my contact lenses. Happy tears and sad tears all muddled together. He reached up and brushed my cheek with his thumb. Cupped my chin in his palm.

"You and me, Bee. That's all that matters. Right?"

I twisted the ring around so I couldn't see the diamond, making a fist so it dug into the tip of my finger. Pain. It still looked pretty, even without the diamond winking up at me.

"A year's not so long," I said. "I guess a year isn't so long."

He hugged me then, and kissed me, and it wasn't until he died that I realized I'd never actually said yes.

· · · · · · · · ·

I have a new saddest day now. And though the ring still clings to my finger, I don't think of it as my engagement ring anymore. *Till death do us part.* What a silly promise, that death could part two people. Death means love grips tighter, suffocates, becomes spiderwebbed with regret. And regret is messy. It clings to you.

Till death do us part. What a morbid, terrifying thing to say at a wedding. Of course, we didn't make it to our wedding, so Ryan and I never promised that death would part us. Maybe that's why it hasn't. Maybe that's why he refuses to leave.

Now, if ever anyone asks about my engagement ring, I pretend not to hear. Nobody likes a funeral, especially when they're expecting a wedding.

· · · · · · · · ·

A golden strip of light shines beneath the bathroom door. I knock softly, twice, then step inside. The man who lives in my shower is perched on the side of the tub, a stack of crumpled white pages in his lap. He looks up and nods hello.

"I didn't know you could read," I say.

"What made you think I couldn't?"

"Nothing. I don't know."

"You didn't think ghosts could read?" he asks. "Is that it?"

"Are you a ghost?"

The man in my shower gives me a half smile, but doesn't say anything. He simply shuffles the papers and continues to read.

I watch him for a moment. Did his hair always flop over his eyes like that, the part slightly crooked? I search for the tiny mole, the one over his left eyebrow, but it's difficult to see clearly.

"What are you reading?"

He glances up. "Your short story."

Blood throbs in my temples. "What story?"

He flips back to the first page. "It doesn't have a title."

Not that one. I grab the papers from him. "How did you get this?"

He blinks up at me like a startled child. "You gave it to me. Remember?"

"I don't know what you're talking about. I never—"

"Who's this guy, Bee?"

"What guy?"

"Who's this guy in your story?"

I stare at him. His eyes look more green than hazel, but maybe it's just the light. I shove the papers at him and slam the door behind me.

• • • • • • • •

"Who's this guy, Bee?"

His voice on the other end of the line was small and tight. I pictured his words with little curlicues of anger, scribbling their way into my ears.

"What guy? What are you talking about?"

"You know exactly what I'm talking about. This guy. In your story."

"Ryan, that's fict—"

"*Who is he*? You always base your writing in real life. You even told me that, remember? God!" I heard the muffled sound of something falling in the background. I pictured Ryan's angry clenched fist. I pictured his leg kicking a chair, knocking it over.

"Ryan. Listen to me. There is no one else."

"Shut up. You could at least be honest." He was breathing hard, and his words were slurred.

"Have you been drinking?"

"Who is this guy?"

"I based him on you, okay? You."

"Liar!" Another loud crash. I tried to imagine what it was. The first time I visited Ryan in Detroit, we went to Ikea, and I helped him pick out furniture for his apartment. Metal stackable crates for his music collection. A long, narrow, glass-topped coffee table. I made him buy the tall painted vase; he kept it in the corner and filled it with sunflowers whenever I visited. Maybe that crash was the vase falling over. I pictured crushed yellow petals, water oozing into the carpet.

"Ryan, calm down. I'm not lying to you."

"I have hazel eyes."

"I know you do."

"I have hazel eyes and this guy in the story has blue eyes."

"So? I just changed your eye col—"

"*Your eyes are so big, blue as a perfect robin's egg—*"

"Ryan—"

"*Looking into your eyes, it's as if I can curl up and fall asleep inside them—*"

"Stop it!"

"*Safe, warm. Protected—*"

"Ryan, I sent you that story because I want you to be part of my life out here. I want to share my work with you. I want your support. I'm up for workshop next Thursday, and I was hoping you could give me suggestions."

"Here's a suggestion. Why don't you go show it to your other boyfriend?"

"I'm not going to argue about this anymore."

"Just because I'm far away doesn't mean you can parade around like a fucking slut."

I hung up. I thought about calling him back right away but decided instead to watch an episode of *The Office*. Give him a chance to calm down and sober up. Then I would call him back. It was *The Office* episode with the casino night party. One of my favorites. After the ending theme music swelled, I dialed Ryan's cell. But by then there was no answer.

Of all my regrets, that stupid episode of *The Office* is the hardest to keep buried.

The last two words he ever said to me were *fucking slut*. That is why I don't like to think about our final conversation. That is why I still eat frozen bread. And that is why I dropped out of my MFA program and stopped writing altogether.

· · · · · · · · ·

I found out later that Ryan had gotten demoted at his job that day. His boss said he had been coming in late, leaving early, missing sales calls. A couple of his coworkers thought he was depressed and suggested he get help, but Ryan never wanted help from anyone. Especially not from me. I tell myself that's why I had no idea, until that last conversation, that something was wrong. I tell myself that's why I didn't know Ryan was so close to the edge. Two thousand miles away and good at hiding. He gave a remarkable performance, at least until the very end. That was the only time I got a small peek behind the curtain.

And what did I do? I hung up the phone.

• • • • • • • • •

Midnight. I can't sleep. I slip into the kitchen, heave open the refrigerator door. Hummus, yogurt, ketchup, milk. Leftover chicken and rice in a plastic container, a condensation of water droplets on the inside of the lid. I close the refrigerator door.

Padding back to my empty room, I notice the golden strip of light still creeping out from beneath the bathroom door. I tiptoe up and press my ear against the thin wood door panel. Nothing. My heart is beating very loudly. I hesitate, my fist inches from the wood, and then I knock softly, twice. Nothing. I slowly open the door and step inside. For a half instant, I'm terrified that I'll see his body, hanging lifelessly from the shower rod.

But the man who lives in my shower is perched harmlessly on the side of the tub. Has he moved at all in the seven hours since I stormed out on him this evening? He wears the goldfish necktie, but unthreateningly loose around his neck. He still holds the stack of crumpled white pages in his lap. He looks up at me.

"Hi," I say. My voice is dry and croaky.

"Hi, Bee," he says.

I look at my toes as I walk toward him. My nails are painted pink, the polish chipped around the edges. I don't even like pink. I sit beside him on the rim of the bathtub. It is filled with sudsy water, cold to the touch. Now my hand has soapsuds on it; I wipe it off on my striped pajama pants. I glance down at the page the man who lives in my shower is reading. It is the same page from earlier.

"I love you," you say. We're lying together on my bed and you turn on your side to look at me. Your eyes are so big, blue as a perfect robin's egg. Looking into your eyes, it's as if I can curl up and fall asleep inside them. Safe, warm. Protected.

"I love you, too," I say. I've said it before, to other people, but nobody's eyes are as blue as yours, and I realize with a flood of piercing certainty that until this moment, I've never really meant it.

I look at him, finally. His eyes are hazel. His part is crooked. He looks exactly the same as the last day I saw him, hugging goodbye at the airport. He held me so tightly, I remember thinking for a moment that I couldn't breathe. As if he was trying so desperately to hold onto something. I should have known, then. How could I not have known?

"How could I not have known?" I ask. Warm tears gather around my eyes.

"I didn't want you to know," he says.

"But why not? I could have helped. I could have . . . things could have been different."

He sighs. "I wanted to be perfect for you. I couldn't bear for you to see me in such a bad place."

He drops a page of my story into the bathtub. I watch the page fill up with water and sink. I watch the ink blur. He drops a second page, then a couple more.

"I am so mad at you," I say. "I'm furious, actually. How could you do that? How could you leave me like that?"

"It was a mistake." Another page drifts lazily down into the sudsy water. "You have to believe me. I'm sorry, Bee. I'm so sorry."

My nose is running, my eyes burning with angry tears. I wipe them away with the back of my hand. "And that's supposed to make it all okay?" My voice rises more than I intended.

"You can't go on living like this forever," he says.

I don't say anything. I hug my knees up to my chin so I am precariously balancing on the narrow edge of the tub. Slight pressure, and I'll fall in.

"Frozen bread and ghosts won't do."

His hazel eyes gleam the same way they did when he told me he was leaving for Detroit. I know his next words before he says them. "It's time for me to go." Only, I realize now, there was something else there before, a flicker of fear that I mistook for anxious exhilaration. That isn't there now. His face is calm. His eyes are unclouded.

"Goodbye." He leans down and kisses my forehead, softly. Just a slight pressure, like the gentle push of an index finger against the small of your back, but it's more than I can bear. I waver and tumble backward into the bathtub, bumping my elbow against one of the faucet knobs and sitting down hard on my tailbone. The soggy pages of my short story, unfinished and untitled—the last words I wrote—drift around me. I glance up at the man who used to live in my shower. He smiles at me from the bathroom doorway.

"Goodbye, Ryan," I say. "I'm sorry, too."

"You have nothing to be sorry for."

"I love you."

"I love you, Bee. I always will." And then he is gone.

· · · · · · · · ·

I have a dog now, a golden retriever. I got him from the Humane Society. His name is Boo, after Boo Radley. *To Kill a Mockingbird* is my favorite book, though Ryan could never get through it. I think he would have liked my Boo, though. He would have liked to take Boo on walks together through the park. We stop at a bench overlooking the playground. Boo curls up on the ground near my feet. He doesn't need a leash; he won't run away. I sit sideways, with my knees up on the seat, and tilt my face to the winter sunshine. I gently open the cover of my worn spiral notebook, smooth flat a fresh page, and place the tip of my pen against the emptiness. It will take a long time to fill it, I know. But I begin.

TARZAN

Jeremy had a sore throat, or so he said. That's how it began.

"Sorry," he whispered when his mother sat across from him at the dinner table and asked about his day. He touched his throat. "It hurts to talk."

"Oh, honey," his mother said. She studied him anxiously. In her eyes, Jeremy sometimes thought, he would always be six years old. "Would you like some tea?" He knew she would ask that. He shook his head, but she was already out of her chair. "I'll make you some tea. How's chamomile sound?"

Just another two years and he could leave, like Walt had. The steam rose from his mug in a slow, brooding way. His mother smiled at him across the narrow kitchen table. The tablecloth had a pea-sized brown stain in one corner. A few years ago, Jeremy had cut his finger with a steak knife while eating pork tenderloin. Four stitches at the hospital. His mother said she would get a new tablecloth, but then his father left and she never did.

· · · · · · · · ·

Jeremy's mother insisted on giving him a notepad for school. It was long and narrow, advertising *JOHN J. NICHOLS, Your Friendly Neighborhood Realtor!* at the top with aggressively fonted contact information. John J. Nichols, tan and Rogained, grinned healthily in a yearbook-sized photo beside his name.

"Here. You can use this to write down things you need to say." She handed it to him. "Your teachers will understand."

Jeremy nodded and picked up his backpack, weighed down with books and binders and gym clothes. His mother moved to kiss him on the cheek, but he turned away; her mouth grazed his hair. "Have a good day," she said, watching from the doorway as he walked to his car, a sea-foam green Saturn that had been Walt's in high school. His mother closed the front door, but as he backed out of the driveway, he glimpsed her face, pressed up to the small side window, like a little girl at day care watching a parent leave.

· · · · · · · · ·

A week passed, and still he was silent. "What's wrong, honey? Talk to me," his mother asked, as the two of them picked their way through another quiet dinner. He met her eyes and smiled as he lifted a forkful of green beans. He chewed, swallowed, and gave her a thumbs-up. She sighed. "Thank you, dear. I'm glad you like it." Her own food turned cold, barely touched.

Later, she found his notepad covered in doodles—curlicues and pyramids, monstrous dragon figures, a handlebar mustache on John J. Nichols—but no words. He was in his bedroom, the door shut.

She could hear music playing, some folksy guitar band she didn't recognize. She knocked twice. He turned down the volume. Or maybe it was just the song ending.

She waited two breaths, three, then knocked once more and turned the knob gently. The door creaked when it opened.

"Jeremy?" she said, stepping into her son's bedroom. The wallpaper was striped green and beige to match his bedspread. *Stripes everywhere.* She thought of jail. "Honey, I found this in your backpack when I was taking out your gym clothes to wash." She held up the notepad. It felt flimsy in her hand. She wanted to shake it at him, but she didn't.

He sat cross-legged on his bed. A book on his lap, finger marking the page.

She sat on the bed beside him. The springs sagged under her weight, making her feel old and sad and to blame. For this, for everything. "Jeremy," she said, tilting the notepad towards him. "There are no words. You haven't been writing anything."

He blinked at her.

"So, you talk at school, then? This silent treatment is only for me?"

He shook his head.

"Why won't you talk to me? Are you punishing me? Is that it?"

· · · · · · · · ·

He knew the tears were coming before they reached her eyes. Her voice warbled, and she wrinkled her nose as if struggling to hold back a sneeze. He put his arm around her. His other arm lay at his side, index finger still marking his page in the book.

"I'm your mother, Jeremy. I love you." Her face was pressed against his shoulder, muffling her voice. When she drew her face away there would be a wet spot, tears soaked through his T-shirt. The familiar awful feeling was gnawing its way through his gut. He hated seeing her cry, but the truth was he hated it less and less the more it happened because the shock had long worn away. And there was nothing he could say. Never anything he could say.

· · · · · · · · ·

When Jeremy was five years old, he watched an animated TV show about Tarzan. Talking to animals, climbing trees, swinging from vine to vine like a trapeze artist through the green cartoon jungle. He wanted to be Tarzan. King of the Jungle.

At recess one day, he stripped off his T-shirt and shorts, shoes and socks, and scampered across the monkey bars in his Mickey Mouse underwear. Miss Clearwater, face like a rumpled tissue, gathered up his clothes in a bundle and led him to the principal's office. It was air-conditioned cold, but he refused to put on his clothes. His goosepimpled legs stuck to the vinyl seat.

His mother was teaching her pottery class that afternoon at the community college, so his dad left work early and drove down to the elementary school. His tall frame filled the doorway. "Jeremy, what in the world? Look at you. Just look at you."

Jeremy looked at himself. He thought he looked the same.

"Let's put your clothes on, okay?"

Jeremy shook his head.

His father squatted in front of him so their faces were inches apart. His glasses were slightly crooked; it looked like they were sliding sideways off his face. "Jeremy," he said, "you have to wear clothes."

"Tarzan doesn't wear clothes."

"Jeremy." His dad's voice took on a sandpaper roughness that made Jeremy cry.

"Why don't you just take him home for the day?" the principal said. She was a thin woman with curly hair that reminded Jeremy of macaroni noodles.

His father stood. "That's probably the best thing," he sighed. "I'm sorry again about this." As they walked across the parking lot, his hand gripped Jeremy's hand so tightly it almost hurt. When they got to the car, Jeremy's father opened the back door and helped him climb into his car seat, buckling him in with stern *clicks*. He shut the door loudly. He walked around the car, climbed in, and shut his own door loudly, too.

Jeremy looked at his clothes in a muddle on the seat beside him. Crumpled socks. Lonely shoes. His naked back itched against the car seat.

His dad cleared his throat. "You have to wear your clothes tomorrow," he said. "All day. Do you understand?"

Jeremy sniffled.

"These tantrums of yours are not going to work."

"Okay."

"Okay then."

Jeremy's father started the car and began to back out of the parking space. When he turned in his seat to look out the rear window, his eyes met Jeremy's.

"Dad?" Jeremy said.

"What?"

"I wish I could be Tarzan."

His father turned back around and put the car into drive. "Well you can't," he said. He reached up and straightened his glasses. "Sometimes you can't be what you want."

· · · · · · · · ·

Maybe it was one of those things she had known all along but buried. Chosen to ignore. Because her husband had loved her. He was caring and attentive, a great listener and a great dad. They had been poor together. Nothing to eat but Ramen noodles and Chef Boyardee for weeks one winter. On their anniversary he'd brought home fruit salad. A splurge. They'd laughed for years about that. No one could make her laugh like he could.

He was her best friend. So she buried the knowledge.

Still, there were times she couldn't help but see it. Once, a couple years after Walt was born, her husband and Vince were on the backyard patio, grilling burgers for dinner, and she looked out the window at the two of them, standing there. He and Vince worked at the same engineering firm. They went on fishing trips and played poker together every Tuesday night. She looked out the window and she could see it there on her husband's face. He never looked at her that way. She had spent the rest of the evening vomiting into the shiny toilet bowl, feverish, her face hot and her forehead damp with sweat.

· · · · · · · · ·

After two weeks of Jeremy's silence, Walt came home for the weekend. He was a medical technician with floppy brown hair, straight teeth, and an almost-fiancé. "Any day now," Jeremy had overheard his mother say on the phone to one of her friends. "He's gonna ask her any day now, I'm sure of it."

Saturday morning, Walt barged into Jeremy's room and tossed a football at him. "Surprise! I thought I'd drive down to visit for a couple days. How's my little bro doing?"

Jeremy sat up in bed and groggily pulled the blankets over his boxer shorts, self-consciously glancing around for Glenalyn. Walt noticed. "She's not here. Let's go throw the pigskin around, whaddaya say?"

Jeremy pulled on a sweatshirt and jeans and followed his brother downstairs. They walked the three blocks to the park, autumn leaves scuttling around their feet.

"So, Mom says you're not talking. What's up? Is something the matter?"

Jeremy looked down, crunching leaves beneath his worn Nikes.

"Listen, if something's bothering you, you should tell me. I can help."

Jeremy pitched the football back and forth between his hands.

"If you don't want Mom to know, I won't tell her. Okay?"

Fumble. Jeremy stopped to pick up the football. The sidewalk smelled like childhood. How many hours had he spent crouched like this, watching ants scurry in their needle-thin lines across the pocked cement?

Walt sighed. "Jeremy, you'd tell us if you were having a major problem, right? Mom's worried about you. Promise me you won't do anything . . . stupid? Alright?"

Jeremy nodded. He flipped the football to his brother and ran ahead, wishing he didn't have to turn back, wishing he could just keep running.

· · · · · · · · ·

"Well," their mother said after dinner, stacking the dinner plates to carry to the sink. Jeremy was outside, throwing a frisbee for the dog to fetch. "Did he say anything to you?"

"No," Walt sighed. He picked at something in his teeth.

"What should we do?"

"I don't know. But he seems happy, Mom."

"Happy? How could he be happy? He's cut off all communication with the rest of the world."

"Not *all* communication," Walt said. "He still nods, you know, and sometimes he smiles."

"Smiles don't equal happiness. I learned that from your father." She wiped crumbs off the tablecloth with a mostly unused paper napkin and stomped into the kitchen. Walt followed.

"You don't have to bring Dad into this."

"Your father is the cause of this. I'm sure of it."

"Mom, it's been three years—"

Silverware clattered loudly into the sink. "I just don't know what to do."

"So don't do anything. He'll start talking again when he wants to."

She slumped against the counter, hands flitting restlessly about her hairline, soap bubbles mixing with the gray hair above her temples. "I only want him to be happy."

Walt shoved his hands into his pockets, thinking of Glenalyn, her goodbye note magneted to the fridge, her empty half of the closet. "Jeremy seems happy enough, Mom," he said. "Happy as the rest of us."

• • • • • • • •

When Jeremy was seven, his mom went on a trip with her old roommates from college. She was gone for three days. He missed her. His dad tucked him into bed, but he didn't sing the song about moonbeams, and he didn't stroke Jeremy's hair until he fell asleep.

One night, Jeremy woke up thirsty. Dragging his blanket behind him, he thumped in his Spider-Man pajamas down the carpeted stairs. Lights blazed from the kitchen. He heard his dad laughing. And another voice, a deep man's voice, not the TV. Jeremy peeked into the kitchen. His dad was standing there with a tall man. The tall man had a dark beard, and he wasn't wearing a shirt. *Tarzan!* He saw Jeremy and smiled. "Hi there, bud. What are you doing up so late?"

Jeremy was too shy to say anything. His dad poured him a glass of water and walked him back up the stairs.

"Is that Tarzan?" Jeremy whispered.

"What? No, he's just a friend of mine," his father said. "Now go to sleep. Be a good boy and go to sleep."

Jeremy never saw Tarzan again. As time passed, the memory took on the obscure haziness of a dream.

• • • • • • • •

"Thank you for meeting with me, Mrs. Henderson."

"Of course, of course." Mrs. Henderson was Jeremy's English teacher. Her mouth looked like a drawstring purse pulled closed. She shuffled papers on her desk. "What did you want to talk about?"

"I'm worried about my son, Jeremy. He's not talking at home."

"Not talking? What do you mean?"

"It's like he's taken a vow of silence, but he won't explain to me why. I want to know if it is something he's just doing with me, or if he's not talking at school, either. I gave him a notepad to write on, but I don't think he's using it. "

"What's his name again?"

"Jeremy. Jeremy Hachett."

"Oh yes, Jeremy. He's been talking in class. I'm sure of it."

"Really? Oh, that's wonderful!" Tentative relief crept into her.

"Yes. I mean, all my students participate."

She felt for her wedding ring. When she was anxious, habit instinctively brought her fingers to its empty place. "Okay," she said. "But I need to know specifically if *Jeremy* participates."

"I'm sorry, Mrs. Hachett, but I can't keep track of everything each student says. I know he's been coming to class." She consulted a coffee-stained seating chart. "He sits right there, in the second row."

"Yes, yes, but does he talk? Does he speak up in class?" She could feel her voice creeping towards panic.

Jeremy's teacher sighed. "Mrs. Hachett, there are forty-two students in this class alone. I teach five classes. Some of my students are failing. Some of them can't write a cohesive paragraph. Some of them don't even know basic grammar. Your son is not one of those students, so I'm sure he's doing just fine."

Walking to her car, her heels thudding coldly against the pavement, she tried to think of what else she could have said to Jeremy's teacher. A sharp retort. Something incisive. Something witty. But words have never come easily to her at important moments. When her husband told her he was leaving, she had just stared at him, her mind blank as a virgin snowfall.

"I'm sorry," he had said. He leaned in toward her, as if to kiss her forehead, but then pulled back, turned abruptly, and walked out of their bedroom. She sat on their king-sized bed. The floral duvet cover matched the curtains. The carpet was beige. She heard the front door open, then shut. She sat there, silent, staring for a long time at the place in the room where he had been. Where he had been standing when he told her.

· · · · · · · · ·

"There is nothing physically wrong with him," the doctor said.

"You can't make him talk if he doesn't want to," the therapist said.

"Just give it time," Walt said.

She tried calling his father, but hung up on the third ring. She couldn't try again.

· · · · · · · · ·

When Jeremy was eleven years old, his mother kissed him goodbye on the lips, as she always did, but this time it made him embarrassed. She didn't wear lipstick, but her mouth felt dewy. Like blades of grass slicked with dew.

"Don't, Mom," he said. He wiped the kiss off with the back of his hand.

· · · · · · · · ·

The night his father left, Jeremy crept into his parents' bedroom and found his mother sitting on the bed, rocking, staring at a blank space against the wall where shadows wavered through the curtains. She did not see him. Her arms were crossed against her chest, and she grasped herself tightly, tears streaming, her mouth an open wound as if she were screaming. But it was the worst kind of screaming, the silent kind, when no sound is enough and there is nothing at all to say.

PIECES

The afternoon I win the game, no one is around to hear my scream
of victory. No one sees me jump up from the couch and throw
my arms in the air. No one sees me dancing around the coffee table,
adrenaline pounding through my veins, thinking that maybe Etienne
is part of this somehow. Maybe he pulled some cosmic strings for
me, getting the universe to align just right for this shining moment
to occur. For the first time in months, it seems possible to believe
that life indeed has a shape, a purpose. That there might be some
underlying plan for the way things unfold—like oxygen, or gravity,
impossible to see or touch but absolutely there.

I sit back down on the couch, twisting open my glue stick to attach the winning piece to the paper game board. And it is then I see that my tired eyes had read the piece wrong, switching two of the letters around. This small paper rectangle in my fingers is not the winning piece after all; this is just an ordinary game piece, a duplicate of one I already glued onto my board months ago. Perhaps Etienne even glued it on himself, in our first few days of playing the game.

My faith and euphoria evaporate, replaced with a familiar leadenness. A memory from last summer sweeps in—Etienne in the pool, splashing me when I said I didn't want to swim, didn't want to get my hair wet. The pinprick freckles on his shoulders and the pencil-eraser mole on the small of his back. Water droplets vanishing on the hot July sidewalk. The memory is so clear, there should be a corner of the world I can lift and step through. Some way I can slip back into the scene. The dry heat. The yellow swimsuit, pinching my neck a little. In my mouth, the taste of lime. A Sunday afternoon. We had made margaritas.

I rip the piece in half and move on to the next piece. My vision is blurry. The smart thing would be to sleep for an hour or two, give my strained eyes a bit of rest. But the game ends in less than twelve hours, and I still have a whole box of pieces to peruse. What if the winning piece is inside, waiting, and I don't reach it in time? The vacant gray space on the colorful game board mocks me. The only thing to do is press on.

It strikes me suddenly, as I scan the piece for the five digits I need to become a multimillionaire. *Perhaps it isn't really winning if you have no one to celebrate with.* But I shove the thought aside, clinging to the belief that this is what Etienne would have wanted. He was the one who began the game. I will finish it, for him.

When the game ends tomorrow, there will be nothing left to hold my life together. I push that thought aside, too. I rip the piece in half and reach for the next in the pile.

· · · · · · · · ·

When I moved into Etienne's apartment, it seemed like fate had brought me there. Not in a romantic way. More in a sometimes-things-work-out way. Before that I was living with my parents, waiting tables in Sioux Falls and waiting for the next chapter of my life to begin. Being accepted into the grad program at NYU seemed like a miracle. I was prepared to commute to class from Brooklyn or the Bronx; no way I could afford to live in Manhattan.

But a friend of a friend from college was sharing Etienne's two-bedroom apartment, and when he saw on Facebook that I was moving to New York he sent me a message. He explained his company was transferring him to LA and asked if I was interested in subletting his room. The building was rent controlled, meaning I could actually afford it. "You can see the Brooklyn Bridge from the living room," he said. I had written down a long list of questions, but I didn't ask any of them. Instead, I heard my voice saying, "I'll take it." The cell-phone connection crackled with static. My heart raced with the knowledge that this was happening. I was actually moving to New York City, and I actually had a place to live. I signed the sublease and emailed it in that day. The funny thing is, I did not feel even a twinge of uncertainty about moving in with a stranger. Maybe that's what faith is, or fate is, or both.

· · · · · · · · ·

Etienne and I hit it off right away. My second night in New York, he invited me along to his friend's birthday party. I ended up dating one of his friends for a while, this guy named Robbie. Etienne dated around, too. Most of the girls didn't last very long, except for Amanda, who I never liked. She would come over and cook dinner and leave a huge mess in our kitchen, and she wasn't even that good of a cook. She put garlic in everything, way too much garlic. Etienne liked to tease me about Robbie, and I would tease him about his women. It was that way between us. Easy. He especially liked to wear this ball cap with the Canadian flag stitched on the front—his parents were from Canada originally—and I would sometimes steal it and wear it around all day, just to annoy him. People would ask if I was from Canada, and I would look at them blankly for a few seconds, forgetting.

Anyway, all of that is to say that it wasn't until Etienne died that I realized I was in love with him. And by then, of course, it was too late to do anything about it.

· · · · · · · · ·

The game is based off the board game Life. It is a month-long sweepstakes sponsored by a big national supermarket chain, and there is virtually a zero-percent chance of winning. That is what I told Etienne from the beginning, but he was a sucker for any type of contest. He returned from the supermarket with the paper game board tucked into his reusable bag alongside the produce and gummy candy—he had the sweet tooth of a six-year-old—and told me not to be a buzzkill, that it would be fun to play. "Maybe we'll win a five-dollar gift card at least," he said, spreading out the colorful game board across our coffee table.

And the game *was* fun, at first. It's rigged to be that way. It sucks you in. Whenever you go to the grocery store, the checker asks if you're playing the game. If you are, he smiles and hands you a stack of game pieces. (You get more pieces the more money you've just spent.) The checker says something like, "Remember us when you're famous!" Even though you know the checkers say this to everyone, it still makes you feel special and included.

At first I felt grudgingly happy to be playing the game, grateful that it was something Etienne and I were doing together. We talked about what we would do with our millions of dollars, and there was a small, secret part of me that believed our plans weren't made of fairy dust and clouds. That they were the beginning of something solid, us dreaming of a future together.

The game board has a START and FINISH, and the directions

are simple—fill in all the game pieces down the Road Of Life, each one corresponding to what the creators have deemed a crucial life experience: *Get Your Driver's License! Learn CPR! Give a Toast at a Wedding! Get a New Stamp on Your Passport!* At the finish line, a huge mansion and five million dollars await. Each game piece has five digits at the top so you know where it goes on the board, what stage of life it belongs to. When you begin the game you're gluing pieces on the board left and right. You're thinking, *This is so easy!* You're thinking, *I'm going to win millions for sure!* That's when the game has you hooked.

I figured out after a little while of playing that most of the pieces are ordinary. Before long, every piece you bring home from the store is one you've already glued onto the board. But you only have five or eight or ten empty spaces left. You're *so close!* You've put in so much time already. It's too late to turn back now.

When Etienne's accident happened, it was early in the game. We had only been playing for a week or so. Most of our game board was empty space. I very clearly could have quit. Should have quit. But for some reason, the game was the only thing I didn't quit. I stopped going to class. I stopped showing up at my part-time job in the admissions office. I stopped eating real meals and I stopped going to the gym and I stopped returning my friends' texts and calls because even typing on my phone required more energy than I could muster.

But I kept gluing on those damn pieces. I made excuses to myself to go to the grocery store, stocking up on canned beans and ramen and Oreos and rice. When I bought a box of a thousand game pieces on eBay for two hundred dollars, I knew I had entered a new level of investment in the game. I told myself that Etienne would be proud of me. Of my passion.

· · · · · · · · ·

"Let's buy a big boat," Etienne said. "Top of the line. All the bells and whistles. And we'll sail it around the world together. Where do you want to go first?"

"Five million dollars would buy us a lifetime supply of Coronas," Etienne said as we watched a basketball game on TV. He sipped from his Corona, reached over to steal a Red Vine from the package on my lap. "And Red Vines. I'll pay you back for this one, I promise. We'll have a whole pantry filled with nothing but Red Vines."

"I know!" Etienne said, sitting up. He was stretched out on the bed beside me. The pure excitement on his face gave me a glimpse of his little-boy self. "We can buy an amusement park! Or build our own!"

"What should we call it?" I asked, playing along.

"I don't know," he said. "You're the creative one. You'll be the brains of the operation. I'll just be the pretty face on the commercials." He fluttered his eyelashes at me. I whacked him with a pillow. We went back to watching the movie, but a few minutes later he said, "I was just kidding, C. You'd obviously be the brains and the pretty face."

. . . .

My relationship with Etienne felt like looking out the window to the first glimmers of sunrise. Just a thin line of golden light peeking above the horizon, beautiful on its own, and even more beautiful because you knew it would continue to expand and expand until it enveloped the entire sky with pink and orange.

What I had with Etienne was just that first glimmer. When he died, it was as if the sun stopped rising and fell backward below the horizon, plunging everything into darkness.

. . . .

The creators of the game have decided that these are the main stages of life: birth, schooling, first job, promotion. Marriage, kids, apartment, house in the suburbs. Send kids off to college, retire, and eventually die at a ripe old age with your children and grandchildren crying at your bedside.

There aren't bad things in this game version of life, not really. No childhood friends moving away. No bullying. No breakups, no bad dates, no divorce. No illnesses. No arguments or job losses or failures or rejection letters or dreams languishing unfulfilled.

No motorcycle accidents.

No dying at twenty-six.

I hate this game. And it's not the mild, simmering annoyance that you can swallow and push down. It's a sudden flood of desperate hatred, the burning kind that makes it hard to breathe.

I want to rip all the game pieces into tiny sprinkles of paper. I still have a pile of them to open. At least a hundred more to get through. I glance at the clock; it's nearly four in the morning. Soon the game will end. Winning boards need to be turned in at five when the store opens.

Furiously, I rip open the pieces two, three, four at a time, quickly scanning the numbers to see if any is the piece I need. The single rare piece I have yet to find is Q7593, *Throw a Big Celebration*. The game creators obviously think they are being clever—find the rarest piece of all, win the game, and you will be throwing a big celebration. *Ha, ha. Not me.*

I rip the pieces open. *No. No. No. No.* I toss them aside to join the mess of discards littering the carpet. *No. No. No. No.* I have so many pieces left to open.

And then, quite suddenly, I just have one unopened piece remaining. I carefully grip it, holding it up to the light as if the contents will be revealed through the flimsy paper. As if what is inside this piece will make everything in my life shift into focus. I squint against the bright LED bulb. The piece is a small dark square.

It might turn out to be Q7593, the winner I have been searching and searching for. Or it might be yet another duplicate piece—*Adopt an Animal from a Shelter! Try a Kickboxing Class! Plant a Garden!*—that is already affixed to my game board. There is no way of knowing until I open the piece and see what it holds.

Twenty-two minutes before the store opens.

I stand from the couch on shaky, tired legs. I fill a glass of water from the sink. Drink it slowly. Stare at the piece, waiting on the coffee table.

The last time I saw Etienne, I didn't really see him. Didn't pay attention, I mean. He was rushing off somewhere, grabbing his helmet from the hall closet, and I was sitting on the living room floor, bent over the coffee table. Gluing pieces onto our game board.

"Bye!" I'm sure he said as he headed out the door. "See you later."

"Bye!" I'm sure I replied. But I didn't glance over at him. I don't have a final memory of his smile, his eyes and chin and fringe of dark hair poking out from under his beanie, his hand waving goodbye. In my memory, there's just the sound of the door closing. His boots fading down the hall. The letters and numbers of the game pieces swimming before my eyes.

I still believe what I told Etienne when he brought this game board home: there is virtually a zero-percent chance of winning. Undoubtedly, this final unopened piece lingering on my coffee table is not the winner.

But I don't want to know that. Not for sure. I want to keep the mystery alive, to wrap the not-knowing around myself and pull it close. I want to keep the door open a crack, even after the clock ticks forward to 5 a.m. and the game officially ends.

I cross the living room and open the sliding glass door onto the balcony. Cool night air sweeps into the room, fluttering the torn-up game pieces. The air feels fresh on my face. Morning smells and sounds are already brewing in the city below: meat roasting, bread baking, trucks rumbling down the street with deliveries. Soon the dark sky will be tinged with light.

I grab handfuls of pieces and tear them into even more tiny scraps of paper. Then I take them with me onto the balcony. At Etienne's memorial service, we released balloons into the sky, looking up into the scrim of clouds, as if that is where he is now. When really, up there past the clouds is nothing but empty space. I knew the balloons were not actually going to reach Etienne. But somehow, it seemed like they might.

Inhaling deeply, I fling up my hands and send the confetti of game pieces into the air. They swirl and flutter around me in a hundred different colors. I watch them floating on the breeze, trailing down into the city streets, looking for all the world like a celebration.

SUSTENANCE

After the daughter leaves, the mother develops a problem with food. There is always too much, or not enough.

Before there was a daughter, back when the mother was young and living on her own, working a series of temp jobs and searching for herself in other people but never finding what she was looking for, back then her refrigerator was empty except for beer and batteries and a carton of eggs, and her pantry was filled with nothing but Pop-Tarts and cereal, and maybe a couple hardened chocolate bars. Back then, the mother went days consuming only stale coffee and grilled cheese sandwiches from Stu's Diner.

She bought a basil plant on a whim because it was a sunny day and she was feeling optimistic and full of beginnings. She washed the basil leaves and made pesto linguine for her boyfriend's birthday. When they broke up two weeks later, the basil plant was already wilting on her windowsill, and the daughter was already growing inside her.

The mother awoke craving a salad with dark leafy greens and cucumbers and tomatoes, the crunch of fresh carrots and broccoli, and nothing was the same after that.

She got a job as a receptionist at a property management company. Stu's Diner became a grease-smudged memory. She bought *The Joy of Cooking* and learned how to dice an onion. She squeezed fruit for ripeness and searched labels for *organic*.

The daughter arrived with her own opinions. She preferred pears to applesauce, sweet potatoes to carrots. She adored Cheerios until, one day, she didn't. On Saturdays, they walked to the farmer's market and filled bags with bell peppers, zucchini, squash, blueberries, peaches, raspberry jam. The daughter grew. The tooth fairy came. The daughter picked the biggest watermelon and insisted on carrying it herself. They stopped at every other parking meter so she could rest. "Why don't I take over for a little bit?" the mother said, but the daughter shook her head and lifted the watermelon to her chest. "No. I can do it." So, they stopped and started all the way home.

· · · · · · · · ·

Twelve summers later, the daughter moves across the country. She lives in a college dormitory and carries a plastic tray around the dining hall for breakfast, lunch, and dinner. She calls every weekend. The mother always asks, "Are you getting enough to eat?"

"Yes, Mom."

"Are you eating enough vegetables? Do they have a salad bar?"

"Yeah, but I gotta go—I'll talk to you later."

The mother eats salads every day, but still there is too much food. In her fridge, the lettuce grows mulchy, the bell peppers wither. The world moves faster than it used to. She used to whittle away entire Sunday afternoons at Stu's Diner, filling in the crossword puzzle. Now even her grocery lists are written in sloppy fast cursive. She eats lunch in front of the glowing computer screen and dinner in front of the glowing television screen, chewing automatically, not tasting much. When her plate is empty, she feels astonished at how it all disappeared so quickly.

· · · · · · · · ·

The mother flies out for family weekend. When the daughter is showering, the mother opens her mini-fridge, hoping to find blueberries, yogurt, string cheese. Instead, she sees the fridge of her own youth.

The mother throws the daughter's sour milk in the trash. She buys the daughter apples and hugs her goodbye, leaving the daughter to her own shopping and eating and not eating.

Home again, the mother sets her bags down in the hallway and opens her fridge. She slices the tops off the strawberries and washes the dirt off the grapes. She sits in the sunshine of her kitchen and chews and swallows, chews and swallows, savoring every bite.

DIRT

Filling his nostrils, cold and moist against his cheek. The primitive taste of it, like licking a grave. Prayers tossed from his mind to the heavens as stray small coins are tossed into a fountain. His left arm throbbing beneath his weight. All around him, darkness. So dark he cannot tell whether his eyes are open or closed.

He tries to roll over, but can't. His hip feels like a bent protractor, all the angles wrong. He thinks of a baseball smacking into the tight webbing of a glove, the mortar and pestle Elaine used to grind spices in the kitchen, puzzle pieces snapping together in a perfect fit. What his hip should be. But his joints do not fit perfectly together anymore.

He tries to prop himself up on his right arm, but it trembles, refusing to support his weight. His left arm, pinned uselessly beneath him, pounds in pain. He chews his lip. Tastes dirt. Thinks of copper pennies, pesticides, worm feces.

Worms. Splayed across the gray sidewalk after a night of heavy rain. There was a song Ben sang, in preschool, about eating worms. What was it called? "Worm Spaghetti." Elaine's homemade spaghetti sauce, a recipe handed down from her Italian grandmother. He can almost smell it, simmering on the stove, tomato and garlic welcoming him home from a long day in the operating room. He breathes in, ever so slightly, and is jolted back to the damp musty dirt. And worms.

In grade school, his class did a science experiment with worms. He snuck up behind Beverly Kimbrall and delicately placed a long, thin, slate-colored worm on her sweater-covered shoulder. Predictably, she screamed, and predictably, he had to stay after school and copy sentences across the wide expanse of chalkboard. Beverly Kimbrall had shiny hair the color of autumn leaves. He wanted to touch it, gently, but instead he slipped apple cores into her lunchbox and chased her with spiders across the schoolyard. She moved away when he was twelve; it was only years later, looking back, that he realized how badly he had ached to kiss her.

The first time he kissed Elaine. Dripping mulberry branches above them, the moonlight like an oil painting. They had met two nights before, at a barn dance. Her dark hair braided in pigtails and tied with ribbon like a cowgirl. "I'm William," he'd said, shaking her hand. Surprised at how firm her grip was. Her smile began at her lips and spread across her face, made her eyes glow. "Would you like some punch?" he'd asked, because he wanted to talk to her but couldn't think of anything else to say. The punch stained her two front teeth pink. He'd borrowed his brother's cowboy boots, and they were a size too small, pinching his toes. Instead of dancing, he and Elaine went outside and sat beside the duck pond, talking until the moon was low in the sky and nearly everyone else had left for home. He didn't kiss her that night. He wanted to, but he waited.

Two nights later he took her out to a movie, something with Fred Astaire. She loved Fred Astaire, loved to watch him dance. Her favorite number was the one with the firecrackers. Fred Astaire wore a collared white shirt with a stars-and-stripes tie, his pant legs rolled a few inches above his ankles. He tap-danced with his hands in his pockets, as if he were taking a casual Sunday-evening stroll, and then the music picked up tempo and in a flash he whipped out his hands and threw tiny firecrackers down onto the stage. Beside him, Elaine jumped with every burst of explosions. When the number ended, with a grand finale of firecrackers like the fourth of July, she applauded as if Fred could hear her.

He was never much of a dancer. His arms felt heavy, his hands cumbersome. His feet never went where his mind pointed. But he tried to learn, for her. At their wedding they danced to Ella Fitzgerald, and he twirled her and didn't once step on her toes. Her hair was swept up in a chignon. Tiny jasmine flowers tucked in, their petals starkly white against her dark curls. She looked beautiful, but also like a stranger. Like a woman in a magazine advertisement. That night, he watched her take the dozens of bobby pins from her hair one by one. Slowly, she returned to her old self. That's when she felt like his wife.

The first time he kissed her—after the Fred Astaire movie. In her front yard beneath the mulberry tree. Her hair hung loose around her face. In the moonlight, with her dark loose shining hair, she looked both older and younger than she was. A woman and a girl. He leaned in toward her. Whispered in her ear, could he kiss her? She smiled and nodded, but her eyes were slightly afraid. He wasn't sure what to do until she draped her hands around his waist and pulled him to her. The tree bark rough against his palms. He kissed her gently, remembering her fearful eyes, holding himself back. Later she told him it was her first-ever kiss. He was glad he had been so gentle.

Their last kiss, he can't remember. Must have been an ordinary goodnight peck. If he'd known it would be their last kiss, he would have really kissed her. He'd have kissed her and kissed her again, and when her heart hiccupped and gasped and then stopped beating altogether, she would have been in his arms, kissing him, instead of slumped silently over the toilet bowl because she felt nauseous but didn't want to wake him.

He was always being awakened in the middle of the night. The shrill ring of the telephone. Instinctual alarm jolting him from sleep with a racing heart. Other times he was pulled from sleep slowly, only gradually becoming aware of the ringing phone. Disoriented, one hand groping around the bedside tabletop, mind still foggy from dreams.

A warm night for April, yet still the moist dirt is cold on his cheek. He always hated winters especially. Having to roll out of bed, leaving the soft warmth of Elaine's body for the darkened chill of the house. Slipping on his coat, fumbling with his shoelaces. Fingers stiff on the frozen steering wheel as he backed the car out of the driveway. Sometimes he felt resentful. Then, guilty. This was what he had signed up for, after all. The ER wasn't a matter of convenience.

From down the street, a girl's high-pitched laughter. A boy's murmuring voice. Loud footsteps smacking the concrete, getting louder.

He tries again to prop himself up on one arm, but he can't move. "Over here!" he shouts. "I'm over here! Help! Help me, please!"

Footsteps almost upon him now—the sidewalk only twenty feet away, across the grassy lawn. But it is dark, and he fell in the bushes along the side of the house.

"You're such an asshole," the girl says.

The boy laughs. "You know I'm just kidding. Hey. Hey. I love you."

"Help!" he shouts. "Over here!"

The footsteps grow softer.

He sinks his head back down into the dirt.

In high school he ran track, the mile and two mile. Without fail, he threw up after every race. Coach told him not to run so hard, it was just a track meet. Sometimes after workouts, when the rest of the guys headed straight home or met their girlfriends at the corner drugstore, he lagged behind. Cool-down lap, two laps, three. When everyone else was gone, he'd give in to his wobbly spaghetti legs and let himself collapse onto the red dirt track softened by millions of footsteps. Sometimes he curled up into a ball; other times he lay spread-eagle, attuned to his breathing as it slowly returned to normal. The very best kind of tired. Sweat cooled his bare skin, mixing with the red dirt. When he finally stood, a thin layer of track dust stuck to his chest and arms and legs.

Those days, he couldn't imagine not running. But then a bullet to the knee ended his racing days for good.

The complete idiocy of it. The needlessness. One of his own men, half asleep on sentinel duty, spooked, an accident. Two years in combat scot-free and then suddenly stuck in a foreign hospital bed. Knee swollen like an enormous bee sting. Then his ear infection. Shots of penicillin every three hours. Pain so achingly constant he began to grind his teeth in his sleep. Nightmares punctuated by groans of wounded men. Nothing to do but lie in that hospital bed. Helpless.

His mother wrote that Matthew had been drafted into the Army. His kid brother and the whole bunch of neighborhood boys, all sent to Europe. A platoon of green soldiers fresh out of high school. Bobby, Fred, J.T. all died at Normandy.

The war ended. He couldn't wait to get home and marry Elaine. Start afresh. He enrolled in college courtesy of Uncle Sam. Medicine seemed like the right path. A challenge. He would conquer the helplessness he associated with hospitals. Banish his feelings of impotence by earning surgeon's scrubs.

Meanwhile, Matthew's grieving heart fell in love with France. And with Marie. Forty-five years he guessed they'd been married now, living in the same small French town where Marie grew up. *Cordes-sur-Ciel.* He still couldn't pronounce its name correctly.

They were happy, Matthew and Marie. Sent letters occasionally and every few years made a trip over for Christmas. He didn't much care for Marie because she never offered to help Elaine with the dishes. Elaine said it was no bother, really, Marie was a guest after all. But he was disappointed. Matthew should know better than to let his wife put on airs. Sometimes they even spoke French to each other at the dinner table. When that happened, he'd kick Elaine under the table. She'd gently place her hand on his thigh and ask if anyone wanted dessert.

"Hudson, no!" A woman's voice, footsteps. The jangle of tags on a collar. A dog's heavy panting.

He tries to raise his head. "Hello!" he calls. "Help me! Over here! I need help!"

The footsteps stop. "Hello?" the woman says. Voice guarded. "Is someone there?"

"Yes!" he shouts. "Over here, by the bushes! Help, please!"

"Are you okay?"

"I fell. I was taking the trash barrels out. But it's dark and I tripped and now I can't get up. It's my hip."

"I'm sorry," the woman says. "I have my dog with me. I need to take him home first. He goes crazy around strangers."

"Please. I live here. Help me, please!"

"I will . . . I'll come right back. I promise."

"Okay," he says. Can't think of anything else. The footsteps hurry away. "I'm an old man!" he adds.

"I'll be back," the woman says. "C'mon, Hudson!"

Alone again. The sound of crickets and the smell of dirt. He closes his eyes.

Nearly every night, he used to dream of running. The setting changed. Sometimes he ran on the California beach, other times through the woods or in the cornfields of his childhood or around the lake where he and Elaine used to go in the summertime, before the kids were born. Sometimes he relived big races from high school, like the time he just barely beat Johnny Galston in the two mile by leaning past him at the finish line. The setting changed, but the feeling of running was the same. Running as fast as he could. Catapulting down hills. The breeze against his face. Joy, freedom. Peace.

He would wake up smiling, but the happiness quickly dissipated. He walked downstairs slowly. Slight limp. Morning coffee tasted bitter.

Since September, he's been dreaming of Elaine. Nothing out of the ordinary, which makes it harder to return to reality upon waking. Sometimes she's sitting beside him on the dream-couch, reading. Or he'll hear her soft footsteps coming up the dream-stairs to bed. Sometimes, his dream-self wanders around the dream-house looking for her, and finding her is the greatest relief he can imagine. He wraps his arms around her and presses his face against her neck and breathes in. She smells of cinnamon and soap.

Nightmares are when he wanders around the dream-house and can't find her. He awakens feeling like his insides were drained away and replaced with heavy stones while he slept.

After the war, they were never apart for more than a few nights in a row. Medical conferences, her grandmother's funeral, occasional school trips with the kids. And then that one time they fought, seriously fought, and she might have left for good if not for . . . for what?

How foolish he'd been. The argument began in a familiar way. He fixed himself a gin and tonic. Sat at the kitchen table, watching her cook dinner. She complained he was away at the office too much. That he hardly spent time with the kids. "You've never been to a parent-teacher conference," she said. "Or one of Susie's ballet recitals."

He was tired, irritable from a difficult case that afternoon. "It's always been a chore for you, hasn't it?" he said. "My career?"

"What do you mean?"

"I mean you've never supported me, not really."

"That's the most ridiculous thing I've ever heard." Her cheeks shone as if sunburned.

"You knew what you were getting into when you married me," he said. "I do the best I can."

She tore fistfuls of lettuce in half. "Well, I'm just asking you to make a little more of an effort."

"You know something, Elaine?" he asked. The weight of his eyelids, the weariness of his limbs. His body sagged in the kitchen chair like a half-empty sack of potatoes. "Sometimes," he said, "I think I should have stayed in France."

In France, at a war hospital, a nurse named Bernadette asked him to stay and live with her. He chose Elaine. Wasn't a choice, really. Elaine was the one he loved. Since that first kiss under the mulberry tree, he'd been hers. But the story slipped out one drunken night. Elaine nestled it deep inside her. Stagnating. Somewhere out there lived another woman who loved him, who he had loved. She said it made her feel untethered.

"What if you'd chosen her?" she asked, more than once.

"But I didn't," he told her. "I never would have."

"But what if you had?"

It didn't matter how many times he told her. And so he knew what to say, if he ever wanted to cut her deeply.

He knew it, and still he said it.

The naked hurt on her face. Her indignation at his apologies. As soon as the words left his mouth, he knew they were irretrievable. Tried to take them back, to touch her shoulder as she brushed past him out the door. She would not meet his eyes. She bundled the kids up in the car and left. Her mother lived three hours away. He tried calling, over and over. No one picked up. He vomited into the sink. Slept on the couch in his undershirt, awakening with a start every few hours. Listened for her key in the lock, her footsteps in the hall.

Dirt on his dry lips. Footsteps. Sneakers? Hurried steps? He opens his eyes, blinks grit from his eyelashes. He can't tell for sure.

The moon peeks out behind the clouds. His hip feels strange, his knee stiff. His left arm, pinned under him, is numb.

That moment the front door flung open and there she was. The sunset blazed copper behind her.

The dirt is cold against his cheek.

He thought at first he was dreaming her there.

Just maybe those are approaching footsteps. Coming to save him.

ACKNOWLEDGMENTS

Thank you to the entire Koehler Books team for their unending belief and support in my book. Special thanks to Hannah Woodlan for plucking my manuscript from the slush pile, John Koehler for making me feel at home from day one, and Joe Coccaro for the extremely insightful edits.

Thank you to the San Francisco Writers Grotto and the Martha Heasley Cox Center for Steinbeck Studies at San Jose State University for supporting my work. Many of these stories were birthed and edited during my time as a Grotto Fellow and Steinbeck Fellow. Special thanks to Vanessa Hua, Tommy Mouton, Paul Douglass, and Nick Taylor.

Thank you to my MFA professors at Purdue University—Porter Shreve, Bich Minh Nguyen, Sharon Solwitz and Patricia Henley—and to my friends and fellow writers for the astute feedback on many of these stories: Shavonne Clarke, Natalie van Hoose, Tiffany Chiang, Terrance Manning, Mike Campbell, Kelsey Ronan, and Chidelia Edochie.

Thank you to the creative writing program at the University of Southern California for helping me build a daily writing routine and find my voice. Special thanks to my professors Viet Thahn Nguyen, James Ragan, Susan Segal, and Richard Fliegel. As always, a big hug of gratitude to Aimee Bender for being my role model as a writer, teacher, and human being.

Writing can be a lonely profession, and I am grateful for the supportive community of my online writing group that formed during the Covid-19 pandemic, especially Robert Aquinas McNally, Katya Cengel, Julia Bricklin, Susan Harness, and Matthew Kerns.

Thank you to Greg Spatz, Caitlin Horrocks, Leigh Camacho Rourks, and Peg Alford Purcell for your kind and generous support of this book.

Thank you to all of my teachers, classmates, and friends from elementary school onward who have encouraged my writing over the years. Too many to name, but you know who you are!

Thank you to my students and clients, who continually remind me of the joy and magic that comes from unleashing words onto the blank page.

Thank you to Jeffrey Dransfeldt for taking such lovely author headshots for me.

Thank you to my family, and to friends who have become family, for your continued support of my writing: Jess Ahoni, Allyn McAuley, Laurel Shearer, Colin McAuley, Kylie Neal, Mary Blasquez, Ann Silvestri, Arianna Silvestri, Amanda Rackley, Julie Hein, Melissa Kaganovsky, Erica Roundy, Dana Boardman, Lauren Baran, Carand Burnet, Michael Swaidan, Ben Raynor, Connie Halpern, Susan

Goodkin, Kay Giles, Wayne and Kathy Bryan, Tavis Smiley, Barry Kibrick, Julie Merrick, Rima Muna, Patti Post, Lenore Pearson, Shana Lynn Schmidt, Justin and Rose Nishioka, Alicia Stratton, Tania Sussman, Henry Fung, Joan Redding, Anna Frandsen, and all of my aunts, uncles, and cousins.

Thank you, always, to my grandma Auden and my dear friends Jewell Butcher and Céline Lucie Aziz for teaching me that love knows no tense.

Special thanks to my aunt Kym Woodburn King for her constant love, staunch optimism, and marathon phone calls that lift my spirits.

Thanks to Grandma and Grandpap, Mary Lou and Gene Paschal, for always making me feel like a best-selling author; and to Gramps, Dr. James Dallas Woodburn II, for showing me the enduring power of a good story told and retold.

Forever gratitude to my mother-in-law, Barbara McAuley, for your fierce belief in me and my writing—and the countless hours of babysitting Maya so I have time to write!

A big hug to my sister-in-law and favorite librarian, Allyson McAuley, who gives the best book recommendations. I treasure our conversations.

Thank you to Holly Mueller, my wise friend and first reader, for always cheering me on.

Thank you to my brother, Greg, for teaching me about patience and faith, and for always boosting my spirits when it feels like the world is ending.

Thank you to my mom, Lisa, for believing in me and my writing— and for giving me the gift of time to pursue my dreams.

Thank you to my dad, Woody, for being my writing buddy and biggest fan. You are the reason I became a writer in the first place, and you are the best role model for finding joy in the creative process.

To my husband, Allyn: thank you for teaching me how to make paper, for taking me to the cabin in Mendocino with the proliferating throw rugs, for all the adventures and tiny miracles every day. I am so grateful to go through life with you. When the world is ending, you are the person I want by my side.

To my daughter, Maya: I love you infinity, always.

AUTHOR'S NOTE

Some of the stories in this collection originally appeared in slightly different versions in the following magazines and anthologies, to whose editors grateful acknowledgement is made:

"How to Make Paper When the World is Ending" in *Flyway: Journal of Writing & Environment*; "Goosepimples" in *Arroyo Literary Review* and *Redux*; "How My Parents Fell in Love" in *The Newport Review*; "Frozen Windmills" in *The Tishman Review*; "How to Make Spinach-Artichoke Lasagna Three Weeks After Your Best Friend's Funeral" in *Your Impossible Voice*; "Receiptless" in *The Literati Quarterly, Flash Fiction Forum,* and *Play On Words*; "The Man Who Lives in my Shower" in *Zahir: A Journal of Speculative Fiction*; "Tarzan" in *Superstition Review*; "Pieces" in *The Santa Clara Review*; "Sustenance" in *The Mom Egg*; "Dirt" in *North Dakota Quarterly*.

CPSIA information can be obtained
at www.ICGtesting.com
Printed in the USA
LVHW101815070622
720711LV00002B/21